Treasure of Taos

Treasure of Taos

Tales of Northern New Mexico

REED STEVENS

Illustrated by Janice St. Marie

A Mariposa Book

Published by
Mariposa Publishing
922 Baca Street
Santa Fe, New Mexico 87501
(505) 988-5582

FIRST EDITION 1992

ISBN 0-933553-08-0

For Sarah and Tammy

CONTENTS

The Serpent's Gift

When Miguel's father died, the boy begged his mother for permission to go out into the world to find work. Although they were very poor she told him she could not bear to think how quiet and lonesome their little house would be without her only child. So he remained at her side while they worked their garden plot in a little village in the Sangre de Cristo mountains.

But the ground was stony and hard and one year locusts ate the whole crop. Again Miguel begged his mother to let him find work. This time there was hardly a bean left in the jar so, though she would miss him greatly, she put frijoles and tortillas into a little sack and bade him a tearful farewell.

Because Miguel was the kind of boy who didn't let grass grow under his feet, he was only a week on the road when he came to a rancho where they raised many sheep. When the estanciero offered him the job of tending a flock on a remote mesa, Miguel accepted with enthusiasm and began his life as a shepherd.

Although he was a self-sufficient boy, a shepherd's life is a very lonely one. For many months the only voices Miguel heard were the hawks calling to each other as they rode the wind and the chorus of cicadas in the summer grass. His sole companion was the dog who kept the sheep safe from hungry wolves. It was a solitary life for the boy. Many a night by the blazing fire Miguel told the dog his hopes and dreams and wished for the sound of an answering voice. But the silent dog just gazed back with tender eyes into his yearning face.

What would he tell me if he could speak, Miguel often wondered. Living as he did among the animals he could see they all had some way of comforting each other, warning of danger or just singing together for the joy of it. Each of them had one of its own kind for company and sometimes many others to talk to. But Miguel's human voice went unanswered.

Surely this dog could tell me many things I am longing to know, Miguel mused, alone under the stars. What smells are carried on the wind? What would the eagle say if he could or the fox or the sheep? He laughed out loud at the idea that sheep might talk. But there was no one to laugh with him.

So Miguel kept company with the sky and the mountains. He slept on pine boughs in a little cave, caught trout in the tumbling streams and snared an occasional rabbit. Once a month the estanciero sent him a supply of beans, cornmeal and dried chili but the man who brought it stayed only long enough to relay a greeting from Miguel's beloved mother and reassure him that every centavo of his earnings was sent to her. This warmed Miguel's heart and besides, he had no use for money in such wild country.

In the spring he took his flock to the rancho where the lambs, now large enough to be separated from their mothers, were sent to market. When the first snows dusted the mountaintops, Miguel moved the sheep down from the high country to warmer pastures in the lower canyons. There the ojitos did not freeze over and there was plenty of buffalo grass to nourish his animals.

It was a hard life but Miguel loved it. He tended faithfully

to the flock, helping the ewes lamb, ministering to all from a small store of herbs and medicines he devised to treat their illnesses. Many long nights he stoked two or three bright fires to frighten away hungry beasts always waiting to steal a sheep who wandered from the flock.

Thus Miguel passed into his young manhood under the bright skies of northern New Mexico. Indeed, he might have passed his entire life this way but for an extraordinary incident which neither Miguel nor anyone else could have foreseen.

One spring day as Miguel was watching white fleecy clouds chase each other across the deep blue heaven, a plume of smoke from the forest edge caught his eye. Thinking it strange that a fire would start with the young grass so moist and the woods fresh with new growth, he hastened over to investigate.

It was a curious sight that met his eye. A small fire was burning fiercely at the base of a young aspen tree. It was not an ordinary fire because, try as he would, he could not beat it out and it burned his arms and hands painfully. More peculiar still was the hissing noise he could not quite identify. As he peered into the smoke and flames licking up the tree trunk he saw a small snake trying to escape the fire by climbing the tree.

Poor creature, he thought, and with a long forked stick he carefully lifted it out of the burning tree and gently set it on safe ground. As he did so the strange fire extinguished itself.

To his astonishment the snake spoke to him. It thanked him for saving its life and begged him to follow it to the cave of its mother who could properly reward him for his kindness. This Mother of all Snakes, the little one said, would grant Miguel a wish.

Now since the Great Mother would grant only one wish, Miguel would be wise to consider carefully what it should be. The little snake advised him in a voice the youth found familiar, as if he had heard it before. The Great Snake might offer him gold or rich lands, the small creature continued, but Miguel would be a fool to waste his wish on that.

The little snake gazed up at the boy who had saved its life. It had seen him walk through deep snow to help a ewe in trouble and keep watch over the sheep through long dark nights. The little snake had seen Miguel feed his dog when there was nothing left for himself and had heard him speak the yearnings of his youthful heart.

"Miguel," the snake said in a firm but affectionate tone which reminded the boy of his mother's voice, "think carefully about your wish. It must be your one true heart's desire."

Miguel's heart's desire. He thought again of the bright days when the birds called to him from the sky and the nights the coyotes sang him their hunting songs. He remembered the times he felt the watchful eyes of forest creatures as he walked among them. How often he had waked from joyful dreams of speaking with them. The years with the earth's mysterious and wonderful animals had taught him much and now, more than ever, he longed to understand their language. And to know if they loved him as much as he loved them.

His whole body felt lighter and the tips of his fingers and toes tingled at the thought that perhaps that understanding might be his. He gazed, rapt, into the snake's eyes.

"Ah yes," the little snake hissed, reading his thoughts exactly. "The power to understand the language of the animals is truly precious. You must ask for that."

A little frightened but quite determined, Miguel followed the snake into the forest to the mouth of a large, dark cave. Inside the cave a huge serpent lay coiled, far bigger than any snake Miguel had ever seen. Its gleaming scales were iridescent waves of color and on the end of its long tail a thousand shimmering rattles hummed and buzzed, making a strange, moving music unlike any sound Miguel had ever heard.

The huge serpent raised her head.

"Who disturbs my slumbers!" she hissed. Her red-gold eyes glittered and burned but when the small snake explained how Miguel had saved its life, the serpent quieted. In a voice like the wind in the cottonwoods the Mother of all Snakes thanked Miguel for saving her daughter's life. Then, just as the little snake had promised, the Mother Snake offered Miguel anything his heart desired.

Perhaps he would like an enormous sum of gold, she suggested. But Miguel shook his head.

Would he prefer an entire kingdom all for himself? Again Miguel shook his head.

Impatiently the Great Snake asked him what it was he wanted more than money or power.

When Miguel replied that he wanted to understand the language of the animals, the Great Snake drew back as if she were shocked. Her forked tongue moved in and out of her mouth several times as she considered his request. Then she spoke.

"The ability to understand us is a powerful gift," she said. "Animals appear dumb to protect themselves from the many harms which humans inflict upon them. We are safest when men do not know what we are saying." The Snake observed the young man who was kneeling respectfully before her. "Few humans are kind and brave enough to deserve this honor because it is not only a gift but a serious responsibility."

Miguel lifted his bowed head and looked the mighty Serpent straight in the eye. His young face shone with longing.

"However," the Snake said in her whispery voice, "you were brave to have left your childhood home to work to keep your mother. And it is greatly to your credit that all the animals, wild and tame, testify to your respect and concern for them." The Mother of Snakes told him she appreciated Miguel's kindness in saving her daughter from the flames. Judging him by these deeds, she found him worthy.

"But I must warn you, Miguel" she added, "there is one condition. If you ever tell another person that you have this power, you will forfeit your life."

Miguel considered this. It would be very easy to keep such a secret for there was no one to tell it to. Besides, he wanted to know the language of the animals more than anything. And so he agreed.

Now in order to transmit this power, the Snake told him, Miguel must touch his tongue with hers. This was a terrifying prospect for the Snake's open mouth was large enough to enclose three Miguels. Telling himself that he must trust his fate, Miguel nodded his assent.

The Snake's enormous mouth opened wide, revealing within its rosy interior two long slender fangs in front, each the length of a man's leg. From the wide lower jaw her crimson tongue shot forward, vibrating, and the Snake's breath brushed

over him, cold as death. Miguel closed his eyes and opened his mouth. When he put his own small tongue forward it sizzled as if he had tasted white hot iron and a shower of sparks exploded before his eyes. But the pain was only momentary. The Snake then drew back her sleek head and recoiled slowly upon herself, closing her ancient eyes to sleep undisturbed for perhaps another thousand years.

When Miguel returned to his sheep, their heads were down in the long grass. But now he heard more than the usual ripping and chewing sounds. To his delight he could hear them talking to each other.

"Look who's finally returned to us," one said. "Our so-called shepherd who left us helpless and vulnerable all morning while he strolled in the forest, thinking only of his own pleasure."

"Oh, come now. It was only an hour or so," another replied. "And here he is back to look after us."

So the flock bickered gently among themselves about whose lamb had been unfairly kicked, why the rams thought they should always have the tenderest shoots and if the winter ahead would be as long and cold as the last one. Very pleased with his new power, Miguel lay back in the grass, quite content.

"Ho! Look at that lazy lout lounging on the hillside," he heard someone remark in a hoarse voice. He sat up and listened carefully.

"What fools those humans are," another raspy voice joined in. "If he knew what we know, he could be living a life of great luxury. But because he is just a poor human, he will spend the rest of his life burning in summer and freezing in winter with only a flock of sheep for company."

Miguel's attention focused on the two handsome magpies preening their glossy black and white feathers in a nearby tree.

"Ha ha!" the first squawked, taking a few sideways steps on the branch and turning its head one way and another. "You mean the gold buried so many years ago right over there under that black ram who is at this very moment taking his afternoon nap?"

"Yes, of course!" the other bird laughed, only it sounded like a scream. "A real treasure abandoned by robbers who never returned for it."

"They swung through the air for their crimes instead," the magpies yelled together gleefully, leaping into flight themselves for the joy of it. "They swung for they hung," was the last Miguel heard as they dropped out of sight.

Miguel lost no time fetching his old shovel from the cave. Rousing the sleepy ram, he began to dig. Sure enough, two feet down he struck the top of a metal trunk. When he had dug far enough to lift the curved lid, to his amazement he discovered a trove of beautiful gold coins. It was a fortune.

He sat by the trunk for a long time, thinking of what he would do next. Then he put a few coins into his pocket, closed the trunk and carefully filled in the hole, concealing all signs of his digging.

First he moved the flock to another pasture. The next day he left the dog in charge of the sheep and quickly made his way to the rancho where he respectfully resigned from his post. The estanciero was sorry to lose him but being an honest man he paid Miguel the rest of his wages and bid him godspeed.

Miguel returned to his village where his old mother cried tears of joy to see her son again. She thanked him for his hard work, the earnings of which had kept her safe for the long years he was away. When Miguel told his mother he was returning to take care of her for the rest of her days, she cried with even more happiness. But soon she dried her tears and began to prepare a feast of the goat he had brought her.

On the very next day with one small gold coin Miguel bought a burro and stout packs. Telling his mother he was going to buy flour, he went back to the mountains to fetch the rest of the treasure. In three days he had emptied the chest and buried the gold in his mother's kitchen while she slept.

As time passed, he bought a few sheep and a parcel of land here and there, careful not to spend his gold so as to arouse the suspicion or envy of his neighbors. His mother was so glad to have her dear son back that she never inquired about the source of his wealth. Because he worked hard and provided fair employment for many people, no one questioned his prosperity. In fact, he was much loved for he was a generous man and had an extraordinary way with animals. When a cow would not eat or a horse was lame, he could cure it better than anyone. He would sit quietly with the ailing animal for several minutes and then recommend exactly the correct remedy. If he could not save the animal, he would make its last hours on earth as comfortable as possible.

While all the village creatures thrived under Miguel's ministrations, the people did not neglect the birds and even the wolves and coyotes for there was plenty of grain and extra meat for all. The birds repaid the villagers' generosity by eating the insects which threatened the harvest and before long the wolves and coyotes were too well fed to bother any of the herds and flocks.

No one knew or cared how Miguel worked his cures. Old people said they had heard of such things from their grandmothers but it seemed ungrateful, perhaps unwise, to inquire. It was better to simply accept the blessing.

The years went by, each one more golden than the last. Although Miguel enjoyed the companionship of his neighbors and the rewards of his secret relationship with the animals, deep inside him remnants of the old loneliness persisted because his heart did not open to any of the many girls who fell in love with him. One by one his friends settled into happy families but though Miguel danced with all the girls at the fiestas he went home alone. His old mother had not given up hope of seeing grandchildren but, as it happens, her life grew fainter until one day she departed to join her husband among the angels. Shortly after this sad but inevitable event, a beautiful young woman named Esmerelda rode into town.

Miguel first saw Esme, as she liked to be called, on a handsome mare, leading a wagon through the plaza on her way to a rancho she had inherited on the outskirts of the village. Dark haired, bright-eyed and hard-working, Esme quickly restored the old hacienda, added barns and corrals, then settled in to farming beside her neighbors. The village could talk of nothing but Esme's pretty house and her horses and especially her habit of riding those horses astride like a man. But Esme's other attributes soon made themselves known. She danced like an angel, baked cakes light as clouds, stitched beautiful dresses for little girls' dolls and simmered broths which relieved many a sick and aching body. In a year her warmth and kindness won the hearts of everyone, including Miguel who thought she was the most wonderful creature ever to walk the face of the earth.

Yes, for the first time, Miguel was madly, joyfully and completely in love. To him Esme's movements were more graceful than a bird on the wing. Her voice was the thrush's lovesong. Her eyes were diamond stars in the evening sky. But more, she banished the old loneliness from the deepest recesses of his soul. She asked his advice and she laughed at his jokes. She listened to his dreams with wide, watchful eyes. Being with her made him feel stronger and more purposeful. He wondered how he had existed for a single day before she came into his life. Everyone saw that he was on fire for Esme with a glorious passion and they were glad for him.

Miguel's delight was complete when Esme returned his great love. She told everyone she considered herself lucky to have captured the affections of such a wonderful person. She, too, had turned down offers from many suitors. Only Miguel, she said, held the key which unlocked her heart. Yes, they would marry and live happily ever after. He would be the sweetest, kindest husband any woman could wish for. And besides, his extraordinary talent with animals fascinated her. How did he so quickly tame the wildest horses, she asked him. Why did birds come to his whistle? But Miguel only answered with a

shrug. When Esme pressed him he looked into her eyes with such intense love and longing that she abandoned her curiosity to the sweet music of his embrace.

After the wedding ceremony and the ensuing fiesta which lasted a week and was remembered for three generations among all the mountain villages, Miguel and Esme settled down happily to live as husband and wife. Mornings he often woke to find his bride gazing into his face with an intensity that matched his own feeling for her. Her eyes were like a mountain spring whose perfect clarity reveals the intricate depths of its beginnings. Miguel felt he saw himself reflected in Esme's very soul. How he longed to tell her everything, to hold nothing back from his dear wife. More than anything he wished he could answer the gentle question in her eyes for he remembered the times when only the wind knew the yearnings of his own heart. Esme would be astonished and delighted if she knew what extraordinary things he had seen and heard because of his power to understand the language of the animals. And how he had met the Serpent, for that was the most marvelous event of his life. But of course that was not to be. He had given his word never to tell. But Esme's curiosity would not be put to rest.

When she once asked why he poured a sack full of bark and nuts into the cattle trough, he replied that it was a special remedy they required. The cattle looked to be in perfect health to her, Esme said. Indeed, they blinked their long eyelashes quite contentedly as they crunched the nuts and when they had finished the bark, they licked their lips with their rough cow tongues as if they were the happiest animals in the world.

When Esme asked again how he knew the cows required this, Miguel told her they had asked him for it. Then he shrugged his shoulders as if he were joking and laughed. Sometimes animals just like a change, was all he said.

Another time Esme watched as he stood by the edge of the woods. The wind blew its soft evening breath through the trees. Overhead, geese were winging their way north. But Miguel was not watching the geese. He stood with his head bent slightly to one side and there was a thoughtful, attentive expression on his face, as if he were listening to something. But there were only the faint honks of the flock in the sky, the twilight songs of birds in the trees and the rustle of squirrels in the dry leaves. When Esme called him, Miguel jumped, startled, and the attentive look on his face immediately changed back to its usual agreeable expression. He hoped he had not revealed the flash of fear that shot through him.

He had only been daydreaming, he said, but no matter how she insisted, he would not say what it was he was dreaming about and stopped her inquiries with kisses. When he sensed a dark shadow in his wife's trusting eyes, he banished it from his mind with images of the sons and daughters who would one day fill their house with joy.

He knew his evasions hurt Esme, yet Miguel could not put the Serpent out of his thoughts for when he did he found his power to hear the animals diminished. He recalled how quickly he had promised never to tell. On that earlier, more innocent day there had been no one to hear his secret. Now keeping that promise was hurting the woman he loved more than anyone in the world. He searched his heart for a way out of his quandary but found none. In a recurring nightmare he began to wrestle with a formless power that threatened to destroy him. For the first time he did not tell his wife about his dreams and this saddened him.

One day a few months later Miguel and Esme rode out to inspect a distant pasture. It happened that Miguel was riding his black and white stallion, a high spirited horse prepared for a race under any circumstances. Impatient at being held back by Miguel's firm rein, he pranced and danced on the path.

Esme's bay mare whose black tail swept the ground, picked her way carefully over the stones, maintaining a steady, calm pace.

"Come on, slowpoke," Miguel heard the stallion tease the mare. "I'll race you to the river. Let's go!" His nostrils flared and his hooves beat a tattoo upon the soft ground.

"This is hardly the time for a race," the mare replied in an exasperated voice and she rolled her eyes at him. Of course, Esme heard only a low nicker. As always, Miguel was careful to pretend he knew nothing of the conversation between the animals.

"It's a glorious morning," the stallion insisted, edging a little closer to the mare. "I know I'm faster than you!"

"Oh, cut it out," the mare replied, laying her lovely ears back and baring her teeth at him for a moment. "Of course you can beat me now since I'm carrying your foal. And the cat told me just this morning that my mistress is pregnant, too, so there are four of us, for goodness' sake, and only two of you!"

When Miguel heard this he uttered an exclamation of joy and reached over to embrace his startled wife.

"What glorious news," he cried as his horse reared a little with the same delight. Esme's eyes grew very large and her face paled. In a cold voice she asked him what he was talking about.

"The child," Miguel replied, "we're going to have a baby!" He whirled the stallion, waved his hat and proclaimed to the mountaintops that he, Miguel the shepherd, was going to be a father. He stretched out his arms to his wife whose horse was standing quite motionless. Esme did not respond to his gesture but on the contrary, seemed almost to shrink away from him.

His enthusiasm vanished. Perhaps, he inquired, there was a mistake, she was not expecting a child.

But he could see from the flush on her face and the way she lowered her eyes that she was. Yet she was not happy. With a sudden chill he realized what he had done. Large tears welled in Esme's eyes as she turned to him and the look on her face caused his heart to crack.

She had wanted to tell him herself, she said. She had wanted to wait until she was certain the pregnancy was safely on its course. And she had planned a special occasion for telling him but now —

Her voice broke. He had never seen her cry before, not once. She sobbed and then she wiped her tears away. There was something different in the face she turned to him, a mistrust which evoked in him all the loneliness of his life before her. He was filled with dread.

"We promised that we would keep nothing from each other," Esme said. "Yet you have many secret sources of information which you do not share with me. Who told you about the baby?" she asked. Her voice was so flat, so devoid of feeling he felt he could hardly begin the answer, could never complete the apology he owed her. At that exact moment Miguel felt his marriage ending and not just his marriage but his whole life. There was only one thing to do and that was to tell Esme his secret. Yes, he would first and last keep his marriage vow to her, knowing full well what it meant. And so, as they rode slowly, sadly, home, he told her, briefly, the story he had longed to share. But he saw that she was so disappointed she did not seem to hear him. When he finished, she remained silent for a long time and only as they came into the village did she turn and ask him, with a terrible despair in her voice, if what he said was true.

As word spread among the animals that Miguel had told his secret and now must pay the price, a gloomy pall settled over the village. Did not every creature owe its own life or one of its flock

to Miguel's tender ministrations? The cows lay down, refusing to be milked. The calves bawled. The oxen shook their heads and refused to draw the plows. Gentle horses turned their tails to their owners and showed the whites of their eyes. The chickens stood on their eggs and broke them. Geese tucked their heads under their wings although the sun was still high. The village dogs stopped their happy barking and the birds gathered in the trees, watching Miguel's house.

As the animals fell sorrowfully silent, people grew frightened. The normal clatter of cooking pots and weaving machines, the ring of hammer on iron from the blacksmith's shop, the rhythmic whine of the sawmill, even the squalling of babies, slowed and stopped. One by one the villagers gathered at Miguel's house.

Esme had been so occupied with her misery she failed to notice the extraordinary silence. Surprised, she opened the door to a crowd of distraught villagers begging for Miguel. He will know what to do, they said. He can help us. But when Miguel appeared, he only shook his head. He cast a final loving glance upon his beautiful wife, saddled his stallion and headed into the forest.

He let the horse pick its way up the mountain. Gradually the sky darkened and a loud clap of thunder crashed overhead but the horse only quickened its stride. A cold rain began to fall as the storm overtook them. When lightning slashed the darkness, Miguel did not recognize his surroundings. The horse was strong under him, galloping now, faster than he had ever run before, yet breathing easily. The hard rain washed away the tears which streamed down Miguel's face. A tremendous burst of lightning and thunder exploded right in front of him. Miguel felt himself flying off the horse, spinning through space and into nothing. His last conscious thought was that he must be dead.

He hadn't been gone an hour when Esme saddled her mare with trembling hands. Her heart pounded as she considered what had happened. Of course she believed him, she had always believed him, except that morning. Her anger and disappointment faded as her concern for Miguel grew. If what he said was true, then he had gone to meet his death.

When Esme swung into the saddle, the mare galloped out of the yard without the least command, following the path Miguel had taken. After many miles at a terrific pace they came to a clearing in the forest. There stood Miguel's stallion, saddled and bridled but riderless. In front of the horse a small snake uncoiled itself and lifted its beautifully striped head. Surely so small a snake could not be the one of which Miguel had spoken.

When the mare halted, Esme dismounted. The snake did not slither off but seemed to wait for her and as Esme came near, it wound its way into the forest, turning from time to time to be sure Esme was following.

The woods were very dark. Dry twigs snapped underfoot. Although the air was oddly warm and still, Esme shivered and pulled her rebozo more tightly around her arms. She began to call Miguel's name in a timid voice, as if she was not sure he would answer. Stumbling through a fog of tears over fallen trees and tangled vines, Esme followed the striped snake deeper into the forest until it turned suddenly, hissed at her and disappeared around a large boulder. Esme wiped her wet face. Her husband was close, she could feel it. But a cold shiver puckered the skin on her body. A strange dissonant whine filled the air and the ground under her feet shook. She peered around the rock to discover Miguel on his knees before a monstrous viper. And this creature, beating its iridescent coils angrily upon the earth and shaking the many rattles of its tail, was opening its mouth to devour her husband. Venom dripped from the ends of its sharp fangs. Miguel did not shrink but awaited his fate calmly, as if he were in a trance.

Esme burst from behind the rock with a piercing cry, ran to Miguel's side and threw her arms around him. In her embrace Miguel felt blood again begin to course through his icy body but the Serpent's glittering eyes flashed fire and a deadly cold wind gushed from its open throat.

"Wait," Esme called in a trembling voice. She stood before her husband to shield him from the Serpent. She let fall her rebozo and opened her arms. The rattles buzzed their awful music but the mighty coils were still as the Serpent waited.

"I can see that you are the Mother of all Snakes. Perhaps the Mother of all Creation," Esme said. Her voice grew stronger. "Certainly you have the power of life and death over the ones before you." Esme lifted her face to gaze into the Serpents flashing eyes.

"I am an undeserving woman but Miguel is a kind and loving man. He has used his gift only to benefit us all." Esme lowered her gaze to show respect for the awesome creature. "And he has faithfully kept his bargain with you, even now."

The Great Snake's jaws remained open but she did not advance.

"Do not punish Miguel for my sin," Esme said softly. "For

the sake of all creatures and our happy people, spare Miguel.
Take me in his place."

The Serpent's head swayed. The buzz of its rattles subsided
a bit. Then the little snake appeared by Esme's side and spoke.

"Yes, Miguel loves this woman more than his own life, as we
can see," she hissed. "And now she offers herself to save him.
This is also the way of animals. When two people are joined by
such a love, could we not think of them as one?"

The Serpent blinked her luminous eyes, rippled her rain-
bow colored skin and closed her mouth. Suddenly her crimson
tongue shot forward and struck the forehead of the woman
before her. A shower of sparks rained down and a thick, choking smoke filled the air.

The next thing they knew, Miguel and Esme were riding
down the mountain. The late afternoon sun streamed golden
and warm over the grass, tinting the green of the piñon trees
with bronze. All around them the Sangre de Cristo mountains
glowed purple in the autumn sunset. Esme smiled at her husband. It had been glorious weather in the mountains, she said,
although she felt unusually tired by the day's ride.

Observing his happy wife, Miguel was grateful that they did
not talk of the frightening events at the Serpent's cave. But he
wished she knew how proud he was to have such a courageous
wife. Then they rounded the mountain's flank and paused to
look down on their snug home in the meadows below. The evening lights of the little houses twinkled in the mountain's
shadow and familiar sounds of the village gathering itself in for
the night rose reassuringly on the breeze.

The mare nickered to the stallion. Esme stroked her horse's
shoulder. They would soon be home, she said, safe and sound.

Miguel glanced at his wife and wondered. But no, her
remarks were only what anyone would say. Or were they?

"Well, it'll be a relief to put my nose in a bucket of grain
and lie down," the mare commented. The stallion agreed and
affectionately nipped her.

"Oh leave me alone, you rascal," the mare told him. "You set an awful pace today."

"That's just because there are four of you," the stallion replied, flexing his proud neck. "Next year when you're only two, we'll see who's really faster."

At this, Esme burst out laughing. "Oh, that horse of yours, he never quits teasing, does he?" she said to Miguel. "Just wait till spring, both of you, then we certainly will see who's faster."

This time Miguel did not suppress his joyful laugh. Was it really possible that Esme knew what the horses were saying? He decided not to ask. All that mattered was that he and his wife, whom he loved more than ever, were together again.

"Oh by the way, Miguel," Esme said with a twinkle in her bright eyes, "it's going to be a beautiful bay filly just like its mother." Then she touched her heel to the mare and they dashed down the hill to the warm hearth of home.

Treasure of Taos

You may have heard of the rich man, Don Juan Cachupín, who married a bruja and died suddenly, leaving a fortune in gold which no one has ever found. Bad luck has thwarted every effort to recover his treasure. One man was killed by lightning when he began to dig. Two brothers shot each other to death in an argument over dividing the loot. Yes, there have been many seekers of the Taos treasure. The last were three young men who found the right spot but as they dug heard such strange and gruesome screams they fled, certain they had struck the inferno itself.

Not everyone agreed Cachupín's wife was a witch. She was never accused of casting spells on anyone, except perhaps her husband who never uttered a word against her, but how else could events be explained? Whatever she was, the treasure was real enough, according to dealers who trade in valuable antiquities and the servants who observed their master's activities.

It was many years ago when Cachupín arrived at the Taos plaza leading a small burro. He was not the kind of person who talked about his past. People thought he might have come from

Mexico City or even Spain but they knew he wasn't from the rio arriba country. When he got to town he seemed to be just another down on his luck traveller but he had a very sharp eye for business opportunity.

He happened onto the plaza in the midst of a ferocious game of trompos, a top spinning contest. It was right after harvest. The hay was in for the winter and the corn had been put up in the sheds. Even the sheep market had come and gone so except for mending fences and repairing roofs there wasn't much to occupy the young men of Taos who were very fond of games and gambling. Maybe it came from living so close to the Indians, the Taos pueblo being on the north end of town. All Indians love to bet and there was no reason why their Spanish brothers should be any different.

Juan Cachupín stood in the plaza watching the youths play 'el corte', a game similar to marbles. In this contest the players put their wooden tops into a circle drawn in the dirt, then each took a turn trying to knock the opponents' tops out of the ring. The losers had to pay a fixed redemption price to buy their tops back and if they had split, which was common, as the game was played hard and fast, the loser had to pay the winner a fine for the broken top as well.

For several minutes this Juan Cachupín observed the lads intent at their game and the others who cheered or hissed from the sidelines. Then he ducked down an alley to borrow a length of piñon branch from someone's woodpile. With a knife he began to whittle at the stick. In fifteen minutes he had made what seemed like an apple out of a piece of the piñon. In another five minutes he had tapered the bottom and carved the top to hold a spinning cord. He tossed a few coins to one of the boys too small to play and sent him to buy a handful of nails. When the boy returned, Cachupín tapped a slender nail into the bottom of the apple, which was by then nothing less than a top, and sharpened the nail's point. Several lads gathered to watch as he wound a string around the top and with a flick of his wrist, flung it spinning to the ground. It stood on its point in a humming blur.

It was an excellent top. However Cachupín was not just clever with his hands, he was also a shrewd trader. Instead of selling the top to one of the many who offered to buy it, he divided the price of fifty cents by the number of offers and raffled it off. While the contenders were busy deciding among themselves how the raffle should be run, Cachupín began carving another top which was good enough to challenge the first. This he sold for fifty cents. Soon he had made and sold enough to keep several players involved in simultaneous games of el corte, assuring himself a steady market for new tops.

Cachupín's luck had brought him to the right place at the right time. When the tops had made him enough money, he and his burro disappeared. When he returned ten days later the burro was loaded with needles and thread, combs and buttons, tiny mirrors the Indians particularly loved, bottles of remedies, pepper and spices, hard candy and marbles for small players. Again Cachupín set up shop at the edge of the plaza and again he did a lively business. Nights he spent alone by the fire in a bare little room, carving more tops and dreaming of the empire he would build.

It wasn't very long before he made enough to rent a tiny shop for his emporium which came to include bolts of linen, pots and pans, whetstones and knives, nails, glue, hammers and saws. At Cachupín's tiendita you could buy all or nearly all of the material and tools to build or repair the necessities of life in a remote village fifteen hundred miles from the capitol city in Mexico.

The town of Taos discovered that Cachupín was more than a diligent merchant. While other men were relaxing from their labors at dances and parties, Cachupín was thinking of ways to make money. He expanded the stock of items on which his customers had come to rely. While other men dandled babies on their laps, Cachupín traded wool and turquoise with the

Navajos, pots with the Taos pueblo, beans and seed grain with the rancheros. In two years he bought the rented shop and the ground it stood on, added corrals in the back and began a trade in livestock. By this time he was Señor Juan Cachupín.

He speculated in land. He leased pastures for his cattle. He financed pack trains to and from Mexico City and even traded gold and silver with those Indians who knew how to find the kinds of artifacts collectors want. Gold figures were his special, secret passion. Not for display, which would have aroused envy and made him more vulnerable to robbery, but to enjoy alone, to possess absolutely. In a few years he had a small but fine collection of Aztec figures, cups, plates and jewelry, all made of purest gold. So successful were his business endeavors that in less than three years from the time he first set foot on the plaza, he constructed a two-story house where the shop had been and it was in its adobe walls that he hid his treasure for a time.

It took almost a year to build and as befits the hacienda of a rico, it was splendidly decorated with wooden carvings and balconies looking up to the highest mountains in the territory. In the front Cachupín's Indian criadas planted a beautiful garden of fruit trees and flowers. This was separated from the street by a magnificent wrought iron fence imported from Mexico on the backs of his mules. Inside, slave women smoothed plaster over the adobe walls and sewed lace curtains for the tall windows. Fine furniture from Mexico and even from Spain decorated all the rooms in luxurious comfort.

Cachupín enjoyed the attention the house brought him. It was so grand people began to call him Don Juan Cachupín. Gossipers said he wanted to be the alcalde of Taos. Perhaps he had even higher aspirations than that and who knows, he might have reached those lofty goals. Stranger things have happened and money is a great enabler. In any case, when Cachupín's house was finished it was fit for a governor of the province.

But in an old town where men are known by their families, even a man who entertained like a prince might remain an out-

sider. The padrones who ate his food, drank his whiskey and smoked his cigars did not bring their wives to his bachelor table. Nor was he invited to their private festivities. As everyone knows, women always played a very important role in the life of properly run towns like Taos. They arranged the marriages, assigned the godparents and divided inherited property. It was the women who invited guests into their homes. No one who aspired to social recognition could afford to ignore the fact that a man without a wife, especially a newcomer, was for all intents and purposes a nobody.

Yet Cachupín did nothing to change his bachelor status but spent most of his time alone poring over accounts or writing contracts of purchase and sale. Every month he unlocked the safe which contained his golden treasure and took out one piece after another with great gloating pride. He rubbed his fingers over the incised plates, then around the rims of the cups. One by one he took up the precious figures made by the 'old ones', golden representations of gods in human and animal form. But his greatest possession was La Diosa del Oro, an unusually fine goddess of an ancient Aztec cult. She was no bigger than his hand. Her arms were crossed over her bosom, her feet peeked out from beneath her gown. The proud expression on her face was finely sculpted. But her hair was what he loved best about her. The long golden braids which wound intricately around her head were actually snakes. He had given a Navajo trader one bar of gold and a dozen of fine silver for the figure but every time he set her on her pedestal, he thought the price was cheap. She was rare, he knew, worth more than all the other pieces together. It thrilled him to touch her golden body, to trace the delicate outline of the snakes, the rise of her golden breasts, her long slender legs.

When the superstitious Indian trader said she was bad luck, Cachupín only smiled. Those cult worshippers were long since dead. She was too old to do anybody any harm, he told the Indian. But she wasn't too old to do him some good. He already had a snake, a frog and a crescent, symbols of a fertility cult disrupted by the Spanish conquest many years before. La Diosa completed his collection.

The servants who observed how Cachupín spent his nights—do not all servants know their master's secrets?—locked in his solitary study with ledgers and treasures shook their heads and said that what the señor really needed was a wife. A woman worthy of a worldly rico like Don Juan might bring a little life into the house and enhance his social standing. But there was no such woman in Taos.

It was in April, the season when bodies are most in need of renewal, that Cachupín went to Ojo Caliente, well known for the curative powers of its hot mineral waters. Indians had dug the small springs into big rock pools and enterprising Spanish

built bath houses for the convenience of paying guests. Visitors could stay in the inn or rent a casita while they took the waters. Two soaks a day relieved rheumatism, gout and other diseases of the blood. Strong gases rising from infernal depths cured coughs and calmed a troubled mind, although too much of the hellish vapor could cause madness.

Swirls of the strange green water boiled mysteriously up from the earth and threw shaking reflections on the white-washed walls of the bath rooms. Cachupín had spent several days restoring the vigor of his aging body, thinking over his strategy for the coming season's trade and considering how best to enhance his financial prospects. Though his business in Taos was strong and his little trove gave him great pleasure, his mind was not easy. His offer to serve the provincial governor as trade liason with the capitol had been rebuffed and the position given to the alcalde's brother-in-law. It annoyed him that his fortune did not impress the padrones of Taos and Santa Fe and he realized that what he needed still was a wife.

But not just any wife. Lying on his back in the steaming waters, Cachupín sighed. His flaccid body tired easily nowadays. A young bride who would naturally want a family was out of the question. Even when he had the strength for it he had never felt the slightest desire to marry. He had achieved the first of his greatest desires, the collection of figures, but now, he realized, he needed a woman on his arm, at the head of his table in the mansion he built for himself to further his political ambitions. If he could enjoy the benefits of matrimony without the strenuous parts, he would gladly make the right woman his wife. She would have to be elegant, worldly and beautiful of course. As perfect as La Diosa, he thought, and smiled at the impossibility of the idea.

The bath was warm, the vapors he inhaled were vile but he was becoming used to the smell. His thoughts wandered. What a strange place the springs were. His servants had begged him not to go to Ojo. They said the devil heated the pools. A superstitious lot of ignorant fools they were. Perhaps he should be touched that they cared about him but he was not. They were only concerned with enjoying the many benefits he generously provided them.

Cachupín paddled among the rocks and splashed water over his shoulders. He had always fancied tall women. Yes, those days in Mexico City he made a regular habit of watching noble ladies take their daily promenades in the Bosque de Chapultepec. Their beautifully polished carriages deposited them by the park gates where they could display their costumes. Sweet heaven, they were gorgeous women. Of course they would never notice a peddler like him. Their hems swept the filthy streets but what did that matter, they had so many gowns, rooms full, Cachupín imagined. Rows of pretty shoes brushed every day by Indian slaves, and hats, they wore glorious hats and their jewels were unbelievable. Fat ropes of pearls, diamonds clustered like grapes, thick heavy gold cuffs, pins, tiaras for their elaborately coiffed hair. It was enough to make a man's mouth water how they decorated themselves. He had never gotten close enough to speak but he had dreamed of escorting such a lady. Cachupín thought bitterly that now that he could afford it, he was far, far away from any such opportunity. He had never had a break, like other men who made their money young while they could enjoy it.

He was preparing to leave the spa the next day when a muddy but elegant carriage arrived at the front door of the inn. Cachupín could not help noticing that the lady who alighted was strikingly handsome and well dressed in furs. She flashed a gracious smile at the innkeeper, then, followed by attendants with her luggage, she picked her way up the path to a secluded cottage. Cachupín sent his manservant out to discover who she was.

The servant reported the new arrival was known as 'La Rubia'. A mature woman, apparently well-to-do, she was travelling alone from Mexico on business of some kind the servant was unable to ascertain. She had been struck by an illness and would take the waters until she recovered. Cachupín's spirits rose. Never one to let an opportunity slip by, he cancelled his plans to leave and immediately sent the newcomer a note asking her if he might introduce himself. She did not reply.

The next day he wrote again to inquire after her health. He described himself as a Taos merchant well known to the innkeeper who could vouch for his means and his character. He asked permission to join her for a promenade after dinner. Again she did not reply. But he caught a glimpse of her late in the afternoon as she made her way up the path to the ladies' bath. She was simply but beautifully dressed and she carried herself like a queen. How long had it been, he thought, since he had seen a woman like her? Years. He wondered if he was dreaming. Discouraged by her failure to reply, he told himself she would probably never have the slightest interest in him.

But after all, he was no longer a poor peddler. He owned herds of cattle and vast stretches of grazing lands, commercial buildings and of course, a very fine collection of jewelry and gold. When he remembered La Diosa, his confidence returned. What other man had anything to compare to that fabulous treasure? He would be a fool not to try again to introduce himself. He had learned how to get what he wanted. If he played his cards right, if he was as patient with La Rubia as he had been in his business dealings, she would eventually reply.

His servant reported that she slept during the day and ate her meals in her room. In the evening she took a long walk under the trees accompanied by a black cat on a silk leash. When Cachupín passed her the second time, he tipped his hat politely. It would do no good to push things. It was enough to observe her clothes, how she wore her hair. What he could see of it under her bonnet was a marvelous red-gold. She left a fragrance in the air. Just watching her made him feel young again. Here, Cachupín realized, was a woman he would consider a suitable wife.

He lay awake that night, thinking of what a splendid match she would make for him. How her beauty and style would arouse the envy and admiration of everyone in Taos. To have a woman like this entertain his guests! Surely La Rubia spoke many languages. Perhaps she played the harpsichord. Yes, the more he thought about it, the more positive he was that she played that delightful instrument. He'd brought one up from Sonora but no one in Taos understood how to make its music.

He allowed his imagination to consider the opportunities she offered. A worldly woman such as La Rubia would surely know how to set the kind of table he wanted to impress his guests. His native cooks would never understand how to prepare the sauces and beautiful pastries he had tasted in Mexico. Moreover, if she was half as charming as she was beautiful, she would have no trouble becoming accepted into the strict Taos society. With that out of the way, Cachupín could pursue his interests.

He listened to the owls hoot outside his window, thinking

how he would make her his own. She was divinely tall, full breasted and small waisted. Her hair, he remembered clearly the hair under the fashionable bonnet she wore, was a flaming red. Her eyes were green, he thought, and he realized he wanted very much to look more closely into those eyes. Her ripe red mouth had smiled briefly at him when he bowed to her. She must reply. He would send her a gift she would have to acknowledge.

He ordered a servant back to Taos for a small jewelry box he kept in his bedroom and when the rider returned, Cachupín sent La Rubia a gold and turquoise ring with his compliments. Although she returned the ring he was ecstatic for she also sent a note, asking him to tea the following day.

He dressed in his palest buckskin breeches and the lace jabot which tumbled down from his collar was snowy white. His boots were immaculate, his grey hair drawn back in a neat pigtail under a high beaver hat. His own gold rings with their precious stones, the pearl buttons at his sleeves, the heavy gold watch chain that spanned his vest, all this announced his wealth. Examining himself in the long glass mirror, he sucked in his sagging stomach and found himself quite acceptable. She would be impressed.

Her maid showed him in to her sitting room. When he saw La Rubia by the bright hearth his heart skipped a beat for her fabulous red hair, restrained only by a silk ribbon, cascaded down her back in the most luxuriant ripples and waves he had ever seen. It caught the lamplight in an extraordinary way, flashing and gleaming as if it, too, were on fire. He could not believe how lucky he was to breath the same air as this glorious creature. But ever the shrewd trader, he made sure his face gave no hint of the joyful turmoil within.

He introduced himself and sat opposite her at the fireside. While La Rubia stroked the black cat in her lap, her maid served tea and biscochitos. When Cachupín commented on the delicious tea, La Rubia explained in a cultivated tone that it was

a special herb she had brought with her from Mexico where she used to live. So, he thought happily, she had lived in the glittering capitol like the women he had yearned after long ago.

When he learned that her health was almost entirely restored, he began to tell her about himself. While La Rubia poured another cup of tea, Cachupín described his business, his herds of cattle, his extensive trade with the Indians and Mexico. He had difficulty concentrating on his story because of the way her hair flashed as she bent to offer him another cookie. His hands itched to bury themselves in those rich, red-gold locks but of course he restrained the impulse and continued to praise the opportunities of New Mexico available to men like him bold enough to seize them. She offered him brandy which he accepted. The cat yawned and stretched, then returned to its comfortable spot.

He complimented her on the brandy and told her how he had built and fitted out his large and comfortable house. Any number of servants stood ready to obey their master day or night. On the third glass of brandy he allowed himself a heartfelt sigh that the house and the servants, yes, the master himself, needed only the tender hand of a loving woman to make them complete and happy. La Rubia smiled enigmatically and changed the subject but he was certain he saw a glimmer of interest in her eyes.

Green eyes, indeed, they were the greenest eyes he had ever seen, flecked with gold. And her skin was fair, there couldn't be a trace of lowly Indian blood in her. She came from pure Castilian stock. He knew he wanted her. More, he was beginning to feel he must have her, that everything depended on it. Not to possess her body. Those youthful urges had long departed. His yearning reached beyond lust. To have a beauty like her all to himself would enrich, even crown, his collection. A strange, pleasant relaxation stole over him. The cat's yellow eyes opened from time to time to observe him. A lady with a cat on her lap. So domestic. The heat of the fire pressed on his body like a strong hand. He must never let her go, he must stay forever in the warmth of La Rubia's presence. He wished he could kneel before her and let fall his head into that lap now occupied by the cat. Get rid of the cat, he thought, watching La Rubia's hands stroke it's sleek fur. He would put rings on those fingers and bracelets on those slender wrists. He would have La Rubia, no matter what.

She smiled. Then she said she was tired and ended the visit. Cachupín was outside, drawing fresh air into his lungs and looking at the early stars almost before he knew it. He returned to his solitary fire and, rubbing his hands as if he had consummated the deal of his life, celebrated alone with a bottle of wine. The next day he sent her a note asking to see her again.

La Rubia received him the second night by the same fire. This time her hair was braided into thick coils high on her head. The light danced and shimmered on these coils as if they were alive and Cachupín again could hardly take his eyes off them for she now reminded him more than ever of La Diosa. He imagined that he was unpinning those intricate swirls and twists, letting them fall over his hands. He imagined he was rubbing the fiery strands between his fingers. There was something noble about the shape of her head as she leaned forward to fill his glass. Like the goddess figure the ancients cast in gold. Again the brandy warmed him and the black cat purred in La Rubia's lap.

She told him the waters had so completely restored her that she would leave in the morning and continue her journey. For the first time she spoke of herself. She had searched for over a year for a place to settle which would be conducive to her health. Unfortunately she had not yet found the perfect location which must have cool air even in summer as she could not tolerate hot weather. Next, the climate should be dry, with little rain. Cachupín shuddered to imagine what raindrops would do to those artfully arranged red tresses. The third criterion was that there must be forests nearby for she was very fond of birds.

Cachupín could hardly restrain his excitement. She had described Taos exactly, the air, the temperature, the nearby mountain forests. Of course, La Rubia went on as if she noticed nothing of his reaction, when she found the perfect environment, she knew she would have to somehow settle herself among the townspeople. She sighed. She was a widow, she explained. Her husband had gone to his great reward many years before.

Cachupín's breath quickened when he heard this. What luck—the situation got better every moment. He leaned forward in his chair with a solicitous expression on his face.

"My dear lady, what wonderful chance has put us together at such a propitious time." He set down his cup and poured himself another drink from her silver flask. She lifted her brows encouragingly. "I mean, the place you are seeking, perhaps the exact situation you require, is nearby. It is Taos whose qualities will keep you in good health, undoubtedly."

"But it is a long way from here," she said. "The weather is cold and I am tired of traveling. Perhaps I should go south again."

"Señora, you are only a day's drive away. It would be a shame if you did not take the time to see it." He must not lose her now. In his torment, inspiration struck Cachupín. "Allow me to offer you my house while you see what the town has to offer. People say the mountains are as beautiful as any in the world. And I have a little collection of antiquities which will amuse you." As he said this, Cachupín determined that La Rubia must never see the goddess. The icon belonged only to him. "I am sure Taos is just what you want. And I can easily find other quarters."

He watched her carefully to see if he had said too much. She put a well-manicured hand to her cheek as she contemplated this offer and he saw she was interested, very interested.

"And how would you know just what I want," the woman asked, her big green eyes intent on his face.

Cachupín's head felt light but clear, clearer than it had in many years. Had he met this woman before? There was something familiar and seductive about her words. The image of the goddess so occupied his mind he felt the presence of La Diosa in the room with them. What an idea, the figure was in the safe at home. He would have no more brandy.

"You must be careful whom you invite to stay in your house," La Rubia laughed. "You have no idea who I am. Are you always so generous?"

Cachupín felt his face flush.

"Señora," he said boldly, "I would be honored. You know

already how you have impressed me." He drew from his pocket a slender box and handed it to her. "Please take this token of my admiration for you." The gold and pearl necklace was a fine piece. Her eyes which glowed with appreciation reminded him of the cat's eyes. It was probably just an effect of the brandy or the fire which was roaring a little as if the wind were blowing. Perhaps a storm was brewing.

Giving his head a little shake to clear these distracting thoughts, he leaned back in the chair and contemplated La Rubia with the pleasure of an experienced collector who has discovered a rare treasure. Her long legs tapered to dainty feet. Her milky white skin was flushed by the heat of the room or perhaps, even better, by the suggestion of his intentions. He imagined her at the opposite end of his dining table, charming his guests. She was a jewel, a work of art.

When the cat jumped down from her lap, wind blew a puff of smoke down the chimney into the room. La Rubia did not seem to notice. Don Cachupín took his leave and stepped into the night. A full moon hung low in bare tree branches, old leaves skittered about his feet and owls hooted in the distance.

By early summer, Don Juan Cachupín could not have been more pleased with himself. How easy it had been. The little town and its dark forest which climbed the beautiful mountains had charmed her. The house was perfect, she said. To his delight, she was very fond of playing the harpsichord. And what he showed her of his collection greatly impressed her. He displayed only the jewels and small plates first. If she became his wife, he suggested, he would reveal the rest. Two months after their arrival in Taos, in a ceremony on the plaza, he married the woman of his dreams amidst gaiety and splendor. Champagne flowed like water. Cooks imported from Mexico prepared food for every inhabitant of the town and the pueblo. Musicians played night and day for a week, dancers beat joyful rhythms on special stages and fireworks exploded in the midnight skies. And to Don Juan Cachupín's greatest satisfaction, everyone attended, from the chief of the pueblo and the bishop of Santa Fé to the governor of the province.

There wasn't a woman for a thousand miles who compared to La Rubia, more splendid than ever in an emerald gown whose neckline set off a heavy gold and ruby necklace, Cachupín's wedding gift. She was a prize of which any man would be proud, beautiful beyond words, intelligent and gracious to all. Invitations to the best houses were coming in before the week was out. The wedding was by every measure a smashing success. Don Juan Cachupín had everything a man could wish for.

When the last guest had departed, Cachupín handed over the keys to the storerooms. La Rubia had set certain conditions of marriage. First, she must have private and separate quarters. Cachupín was relieved and delighted. Next, she would tolerate no dogs on the property for the sake of her cat. Cachupín did not care for either dogs or cats so he made no protest about that.

Thirdly, she must be in charge of all housekeeping tasks, including lighting the fires and cooking. No one could enter the kitchen without her permission where she must be the absolute authority. Cachupín considered that a reasonable request as long as the food was as good as or better than his Indian slaves could prepare.

And so they settled down together, Cachupín busy with his transactions and La Rubia in charge of the housekeeping. Evenings when they were not dining out, they sat in the salon. If he requested it, La Rubia would take her place before the keyboard of the little harpsichord and play Bach or Vivaldi with such skill and passion Cachupín felt himself transported into another realm. But her repertoire was not limited to modern works. She also composed her own music, melodies and chords which evoked the haunting sounds and colors of the noble Spanish and ancient Indian empires. When La Rubia performed for his guests, Cachupín's pride in his talented new acquisition knew no bounds and he was happy.

It was not until a few months had passed that he noticed anything unusual about his life with La Rubia. And they were only trivial matters. The way the harpsichord seemed to play by itself when there was no one in the room disturbed Cachupín but he told himself he was only remembering music from the night before. And it seemed extravagant to Cachupín that a fire be lit in every hearth even when the day was warm and La Rubia became upset if one went out.

It was amusing but strange how dogs ran from her. Even the most persistent yapping mutt whined and hid when she passed by. There were other things, the occasional mistakes made, for example, about where she was seen. At dinner one evening the mayor's wife remarked how diligently La Rubia had collected mushrooms high on the mountain the same day Cachupín had dined with his wife at that very hour at home. Could the beautiful La Rubia have a double in Taos? This ridiculous mistake engendered much laughter, especially from La Rubia. Another time a lad delivered a side of venison he claimed the lady had ordered in person that morning when Cachupín was certain his wife was asleep in her suite.

Her peculiar habit of occasionally sleeping beyond noon irritated Cachupín although he told himself he had eaten a bachelor breakfast for almost sixty years. He could not imagine why she stayed in bed with the curtains drawn for hours after the rest of the world was up and about its business. She said she was not ill but offered no excuses. On these mornings Cachupín found his toast hot, tea ready and a newly kindled fire burning brightly but no sign of his wife or any other soul in the kitchen, except the cat who never left the hearth. His dislike for the cat grew stronger every time he saw it. He told himself that one day he would have her get rid of it but the days passed and he always seemed to forget to mention this to his wife.

It was the cat who precipitated the most peculiar events. On those occasional evenings when they were alone, Cachupín retired to his private office after dinner and locked the door

behind him. Taking a key from his waistcoat he opened a drawer in his desk. With the key he found there he opened a safe in the wall behind a rare painting of the Virgin La Conquistadora. He had promised La Rubia she would see his collection but he did not mean to show her every item at once and never the goddess. Only he would ever see La Diosa, she was his alone.

On these evenings, Cachupín would remove one object, then close and secure the locks before taking the golden figure downstairs to the salon where La Rubia waited. He had installed the safe himself at midnight during the construction of the house and he intended that no one would ever see him perform this secret opening ritual. Thus he was very startled the night he turned from the safe to find the cat sitting by the hearth watching him with its wide yellow eyes.

Cachupín angrily opened a window and grabbed for the cat to throw it out. But the cat leaped at his hand with a terrible snarl and sank its long teeth into his palm. Enraged, Cachupín howled, jumped back and reached for the hearth poker but to his amazement and dismay found he could not lift it. Desperate with pain he searched for an object to throw, seized a crystal paperweight from his desk and hurled it with all his might. The paperweight struck the cat full in the face and with a noise like a small cannon shattered into a thousand brilliant lights. But when the shards had settled, there was no sign of the cat, only an owl feather on the floor by the window. However thoroughly Cachupín searched the room there was nothing but his bloody hand to show the cat had been there at all.

More angry than he could ever remember being, Cachupín wrapped his hand in a kerchief. He poured himself a brandy and sat for a long moment by the fire. The crystal shards twinkled in the lamplight from every corner of the room but he could see no cat, injured or otherwise. He reached again for the poker which had seemed too heavy to lift but this time it came out of its stand like a perfectly normal tool meant to move burning logs in the fire.

The room below where La Rubia quietly waited was the same serene room he had left. There she sat, a model of domesticity, stitching beads onto a strip of fabric. She looked up with a smile on her face, her eyes alight with pleasure at seeing him, then concerned at the reddening bandage on his hand. She said nothing but left immediately and returned with materials to clean the wound. Cachupín's anger diminished only slightly as she spread a soothing unguent on his hand. The bleeding and even the pain subsided instantly. She bandaged him and brought him a fresh brandy.

He broke the silence first. He would shoot the cat, he said, in the morning. La Rubia sighed and shrugged her shoulders. If he could get his hands on the cat he would shoot him that night, Cachupín went on. He hated the cat. Talking about the cat made him even angrier. The cat must die. Cachupín imagined roasting the cat alive. Yes, in the morning he would catch it in a sack and he, Cachupín himself, would slowly roast it over the coals in the fireplace. He would like very much to hear its tormented howls.

"You will bring me the cat in the morning," he said to La Rubia. Yes, that would avenge him. "And I shall dispose of it."

She shook her head slightly and continued to sew.

"You may not kill the cat," she said calmly. "It is mine. You must not even touch it."

Cachupín looked at La Rubia with disbelief. Was this not his house and she his wife? Her authority could never supersede his. He was more determined than ever the cat must go.

"How dare you tell me what I may not do in my own house?" he snapped. "No woman speaks to me like that."

"Perhaps no woman does. But there are certain things you do not understand, Don Juan," she interrupted as the room warmed uncomfortably. He wished she had not put so much wood on the fire. "Do you remember what you told me about your golden figures?" she continued. He nodded, with the image of La Diosa strongly in his mind. He had extolled the beauty and value of the collection but he had never mentioned the goddess, not specifically. He never would. He tried to banish La Diosa from his mind but he seemed unable to concentrate on anything else. The fire was so warm and it was darker by the minute. La Diosa waited upstairs in the safe in the wall and the key was in his pocket.

He set the golden figure of a frog before La Rubia.

"Have I not shown you everything I promised?" he asked, indicating the object.

"I wonder," she replied, glancing briefly at the frog. "When you asked me to become your wife for reasons of your own which I well understood, you made certain promises. You boasted that you owned some very rare icons but you have only shown me minor artifacts. I think it's time you let me see the real treasure."

The sound of a door slamming shut in the kitchen interrupted her. She excused herself. Cachupín laid his head on the back of the chair and breathed deeply. He had bragged about his collection but he hadn't described La Diosa in a specific way. Or had he? How else could La Rubia know about her? Perhaps she sent the cat to spy on him. Before he met La Rubia he would have said such a thing was impossible but things were not as plain and straightforward as they had been. Women were too complicated and confusing. It seemed the marriage was a mistake but what to do about it now? There was no pain in his hand but he felt extraordinarily tired. La Rubia bade him good night from the doorway and went upstairs. Cachupín sat a while, then returned to his study. As he put the golden frog away he was surprised to see that the broken crystal had been swept away. But he was even more surprised to see the crystal paperweight itself perfectly intact in its usual place on his desk. Was he going mad? He sighed. Tomorrow he would dispose of the cat.

The next morning Cachupín found his tea and toast ready at his place in the dining room and La Rubia in the kitchen kneading dough for bread. The black cat sat as usual on the hearth as if nothing had happened, watching him. Surprised, Cachupín said little and after eating went out of the house to attend to business.

But his business that morning was the purchase of two stout canvas sacks with heavy strings on their necks and when La Rubia left the rising bread to attend to her shopping, Cachupín returned to the kitchen. Wearing heavy gloves he grabbed the unresisting cat, thrust it into the bag and drew the string tight. Then he threw the bag into the fire, turned and went upstairs. In a few moments he came down clutching the second sack to his chest, mounted his horse and rode away.

He expected a tirade from his wife when he returned that evening but apparently she had not noticed the cat was missing. In fact, she was reassuringly solicitous of him, asking if he liked the unusual roast she had prepared with his favorite potatoes and a delicious pudding for dessert. She filled his wine glass many times and laughed at his witty way of describing how he came to make his fortune on the Taos plaza. What fools they were, he told her, those lads who spun their tops never noticing how he profited from their simple-minded pastime. It was so easy to make a fortune on the gullibility of stupid people, certainly less work than following a plow or chasing cattle. The trick was to see what people wanted and find a way to make it pay. La Rubia said she agreed completely.

She took his arm to steady him from the table to the salon. It was wonderful to have such a supportive and steady wife to lean on, he told her, one who understood him so well. One who didn't mind if he drank a little too much wine with her truly delicious dinner. She was a joy and a pleasure to have in his house, had he told her that lately?

La Rubia shook her head but she was smiling. Cachupín longed to reach up to touch, only touch, nothing more, her shining hair. He raised his hand but he was too tired to finish the gesture and collapsed heavily into a chair. The tray of brandy and glasses was at hand. She poured for both of them. How good he felt, better than he had in years. Very tired but warm, relaxed, safe. There it was, a wild Indian melody from the harpsichord although she was not sitting on the bench. No matter how the thing played, it was a sweet nostalgic music. He wanted to tell his wife, his pretty wife, how much he enjoyed seeing her by his hearth but the words wouldn't come. And that he was sorry for something, what was it? Something he had done to her, something mean, that very morning. Oh, the cat, he began to say but she was shushing him and coming towards him and she was unpinning that beautiful braid. Sweet heaven, he could feel it brush his cheek as she leaned over him and put her hands on his face, her cool hands caressed his cheeks, her hair fell down all around, he was lost in its luxurious silken curtains, not at all like snakes but sweet woman's hair. And her hands were softly touching his face and shoulders and then, he had never felt anything like it, they were in his clothing, pressing his chest and his arms and under his arms and then a sweet chord of happiness swept him up and carried him away to a beautiful place.

La Rubia took the key from Cachupín's vest pocket and opened the drawer in his desk. Just as the cat said, the second key opened the safe behind La Conquistadora. And inside the safe La Rubia found the one piece of the treasure Cachupín had not buried that day because, strangely, he had not been able to lift it from its pedestal. La Rubia sighed when she saw La Diosa for it was what she had come so many miles over so many years to acquire.

"Now I will take you home, Mother," she said as she wrapped the goddess in a shawl and went downstairs. Cachupín slept like a child in the chair. She replaced the key in his vest, laid her hands on his head one last time almost as if she were sorry to leave him, then turned away.

Early the following day a band of hunters on the mountain shot a man. It was a mistake of course. No one could explain how it happened. A huge old elk came toward them, they reported, bellowing softly. It was not an unusually long shot. Three men took aim and dropped him but when they found the carcass, it was the body of Cachupín.

More peculiar still was the disappearance of his beautiful wife. The rooms of the house were neat and tidy and even the hearths were swept completely clean of ashes. The only unusual things anyone found were two owl feathers on the kitchen floor but that's not really so odd, there have always been plenty of owls around Taos. There was also the low note, more a vibration, from the harpsichord, as if La Rubia's foot were still on the continuo pedal.

Don Juan Cachupín's safe, when it was eventually found, contained all the jewels he had given his wife and his papers, but no gold. The servants had seen him ride away with a heavy saddlebag the day before he died. Some speculated that La Rubia saw where he buried his beautiful golden figures and he killed her to keep her from stealing them. But if she really was a bruja, she took only one piece for she couldn't carry any more than that in the talons of an owl.

Many say she served him the cat for dinner that night and that was how she changed Cachupín into an elk. The poor creature in the forest was searching for her. The old stories raise many questions, que no? But you'll have to find the answers, and the treasure, yourself.

San Christóbal's Sheep

Las Trampas was not unusual in its poverty, for in the days when the Spanish pobladores first settled in northern New Mexico all the mountain villages were poor and Indian raids made their lives almost unbearable. Often only their faith gave them the strength to endure.

So it happened that one autumn day Filipa was grinding corn outside the door of the little adobe house she and her husband had built. She was gathering the pale yellow atole into an olla when a shout from her husband turned her blood to ice.

"Indians!" he yelled, running hard into the yard, picking the sickle off it's peg on the wall. "Quick, into the cellar!"

Filipa would never forget her husband's face, slick with sweat, pale with fear. The curved blade of the sickle in his hand was a dull blue. It would soon be red with human blood, she knew, because in spite of the villagers' prayers to the saints, the evil was coming again.

Her husband tucked an axe into his belt. One small sickle and a clumsy woodcutting axe, poor weapons against the Utes' sharp arrows which could pierce a cow. And the tomahawks.

The hair on her head lifted. She was not breathing. Then she remembered.

"Lupe!" she whispered, hoarse now in her fear. "I sent her to Archuleta's." The girl had taken a pot of soup to the sick family. "She's not back—"

Her husband lifted the cover of the trap door in the dirt floor just inside the little house and gestured impatiently for her to get in.

"Don't worry," he snapped. "I'll bring her to you. Now hurry, they're almost here!"

As if she were in a dream Filipa obediently entered the hole her husband had made for just such a purpose. He dropped the cover and kicked dirt over it to conceal it. It had worked before, perhaps it would work again. Filipa drew a breath of the cold, earthy air and waited.

She waited but Lupe did not come.

Perhaps it was a mistake and this time the Indians were friendly traders. Their ponies would be loaded with furs and leather bags of turquoise beads. Even though the people of Trampas had no money, they could exchange their vegetables or fine ground atole for a small hide. Two years ago her husband had given a fresh nanny goat for a bearskin and she had made Lupe the loveliest boots.

When Filipa heard the first howl her skin crawled with dread and she swallowed her rising nausea. She must not allow herself to think about the Indians who were at that moment drawing back the strings of their bows, lifting their big knives, faces as hideous as fiesta masks. Hot tears spurted from her eyes. She ground them away with the heel of her hand.

Let it be a trading party, she prayed. But the muffled beat of galloping hooves and the screams that reached her ears meant this was no trading party. It was the Utes again.

The rapacious Utes were not like the peaceful Indian people down along the great river who were too busy farming their crops to make war. The pueblos were well defended by the

Governor's Army. Filipa envied women whose children could safely mind the flocks, women protected by many strong men. She often dreamed of a wide green valley where happy children sang and played. That would be Heaven, she thought. But it was only a dream and dreams did not come true.

Filipa did not understand why the Utes and the Apaches hated them. The Spanish had built their houses on land the Indians never used, except for hunting. Surely God intended His people to live peacefully together, work hard and keep the Holy Faith. Does God intend that I hide in the dark like a mouse, she mused bitterly. Why does He let people kill each other?

Even her hands over her ears could not stop the terrible sounds that penetrated the little cellar. She should say a prayer for all the souls who were now rising up to Heaven. She should say a prayer of thanksgiving that she was still alive. But she would not. The Holy Mother suffered for the sins of the world, the priest taught. But it was not enough to stop the pain. Nothing stopped the slaughter. No, Filipa would not pray.

Then it was quiet. She should go out now and look for Lupe. But instead, in the blackness Filipa curled up like a baby and imagined that Lupe was still inside her belly, safely unborn. Her only child, a blessing. Others had come to them but died as infants and then there were no more. But Lupe was so loving and beautiful and clever, so perfect she made up for all the brothers and sisters she would never have.

She had learned how to milk the goat, grind the corn, make the thinnest tortillas, even sew a straight hem, although she was only seven years old. Lupe had also learned the songs of the mountain people, songs of true love even death could not vanquish. When Lupe sang, people wept. Behind the pounding of her own blood Filipa remembered the sound of that voice, pure and sweet as a flute. Lupe had already sung at many wedding parties.

"She's just like her mother," Filipa's husband always said

and he hugged them both at once. Lupe was also kind to other children and most gentle with animals. Her father's dog had adored her and protected her since she was only a baby. In the dark, Filipa wept for her daughter and her fine husband, her little house, her happy life.

She had no way of telling how much time had passed since the door dropped over her but she could not postpone the awful truth any longer. She prepared herself for the worst. She was certain the goats and sheep would be gone and perhaps the brave dog who would fight valiantly to protect them. She hardened herself. The village might be ashes.

She pushed up the heavy door. It was nearly evening. The air smelled of blood and smoke and something else. Charred flesh. They had burned several barns and taken the sheep again. When Filipa stepped carefully outside, she could hear the cries of the injured.

Her husband lay dead on his back by the gate to the corrals, an arrow through his chest, another in his thigh. The blood of the mangled dog lying nearby had pooled with his master's. Neither the sickle nor the axe were anywhere to be seen. They have stolen even the tools of our livelihood, Filipa thought. They take our lives and then they take everything else. Where is God in this, she asked, feeling the flames of pain and rage rise inside her. There is no God, not in this world. Blasphemy, yes, but what did it matter? She knelt by her husband's body and closed his eyes.

"Oh dearest one, surely you did not mean to leave me so alone," she sobbed onto his stiffening chest.

Alone indeed for though Filipa trudged through the village calling her child in a weeping voice, Lupe was nowhere to be found. The Utes had taken her, too.

When winter set in, Filipa lived with the Sanchez family who had lost a husband and two sons in that raid. The women shared a few beans and corn the Indians had not found. It was lonely at night without even the comfort of the dog. Filipa ate as little as possible of the scanty rations. With no child and no husband, there was no reason to eat. There was no reason to live.

When the year turned and the forgetful lilacs bloomed, Filipa returned to her empty house and her own field. There were so few left strong enough to work and the village needed every bean, every squash. But there was no joy in this season of renewal. From a sack of borrowed seed, Filipa planted from fence to fence, fiercely jabbing the beans into the ground. Her hoe struck sparks on the stones. She worked from sunrise until long after sunset. She did not count the lengthening days nor hear the birds' nesting songs but kept entirely to herself.

She no longer blessed herself when she passed the church on some errand. She tried not to see the small cross above the belfry bent a little to one side by the wind. She let it all go, the daily stations of the cross, vespers, even the priest's masses. The saints in their nichos by the altar could wait until Hell froze over to see her on her knees. Her heart had hardened into stone. Without anyone to care for, she was nothing, not a human being, just another mouth for the village to feed. She would work until she dropped and she hoped it would be soon. Nights she did not build a fire in the fireplace to warm her food. She liked the cold. She would soon be even colder.

She did not bother to wash her clothing or wear her bonnet because it was too much trouble to tie the strings. Her skin burned and weathered and her hands, blackened with earth, cracked and bled. She was as thin as a ghost. With grim satisfaction she noticed that she was disappearing. Alone she hoed and weeded the bean field and shoveled mud from the acequia to keep the water flowing through the ditch into the furrows.

Her beans sprouted in thick green lines. About the time they set their first blossoms, Juan Vigil, the detestable Juan Vigil of no family and brutish disposition, a man who had proclaimed his undying devotion to each of the village maidens and been soundly rejected by all, began to pay court to Filipa.

Filipa knew immediately on what basis he presumed to offer her his unwanted attention. Only his sheep had been spared the autumn raid, being on the mesa top when the Utes came. Now he proclaimed himself the richest man in the village. On this feeble authority, when he drove his flock past her farm, he called to her.

She did not lift her head to acknowledge him. How dare he intrude his crude bragging voice into her silence. He leaned on her rickety fence and called her again. How dare he speak the name of a person who used to be wife and mother, a woman who once was capable of love. That person was dead, lost with Lupe somewhere on the wind. Filipa would not permit him to invoke those precious golden days. She did not answer.

As his flock nibbled the verge he rocked a loose fence post. He could honey his coarse voice but to Filipa he was worse than swine, she muttered to herself as she bent over the rows picking off the hungry grasshoppers. Juan Vigil was mud beneath her feet. She moved away, ignoring him.

Perhaps this irritated him. He called her name again and when he saw she would not answer he grew bolder and added words like sweetheart and beautiful to it. She closed her ears but every day he stopped to call. If she could, she stayed inside the house, although it angered her to have to hide. He knew where she was so he waited, whistling loudly, until his sheep became anxious to move on to graze. When she did not show herself, he made water on the corners of her fence like an animal marking his territory. Her rage grew.

One Saturday he followed her to the plaza market. As she spread her blanket and arranged her chiles and herbs, he stood next to her and hawked her wares as if he were already her husband. The village saw what he was doing but no one tried to stop him. What could anyone say? Each had her own grief to mind. It was Filipa's business.

For a month Juan Vigil courted Filipa, bolder every day. First he promised he would wait forever for her hand in holy

matrimony. Then he promised her a warm house and many children. Next he predicted she would forget her husband and her child. Finally he declared that she must forget her husband and Lupe. When Filipa raised her eyes at this to look at him, he grinned confidently. She approached him, unblinking.

"You pig," she said through clenched teeth. "I would not wipe my boots on you. Everyone knows you heard the Utes that day. How could you not? While they were killing us, you hid in the mountains. You do not deserve to live." When she finished, she spat in his face.

Juan Vigil was taken aback. Wiping his cheek with his sleeve, he glanced around in case someone might have witnessed the insult. Yes, the Sanchez children were coming down the road with wood. They had stopped, frightened. Soon the whole village would know how Filipa had answered his invitation to matrimony.

The next time Juan Vigil drove his sheep past Filipa's bean field, he pushed down a section of her fence and let a few sheep in to graze. When she came out, he sent his dogs in to retrieve the sheep.

"You'll be sorry if you don't marry me," he called to her. She only set to fixing the fence. The wood was soft with rot but she did not have the strength to go to the forest to cut fresh posts.

The next day Vigil called her to watch as he let a few more sheep into her beans. This time she threw stones at the sheep and at him. The stones fell at his feet. Vigil laughed.

On the third day, Vigil let the entire flock into her field and shook his big shepherd's crook at the women and children who gathered to help Filipa drive them out. When his dogs showed their teeth at the women, Vigil laughed again. In an hour or so the sheep had eaten most of the beans so Vigil took them up the little road to their daily pasture.

That afternoon marked the first time in nearly a year that Filipa had entered the church. San Christóbal gazed down upon her with painted eyes. In one hand he held a crucifix, with the other hand he pointed to a road that wound off into a painted landscape. This retablo of the saint was the greatest treasure in the village, after the church itself. The small wooden painting stood in its own alcove to the right of the Virgin's altar. Many people had left offerings to San Christóbal on the plank below the nicho: faded flowers, a wedding ring, a scrap of ribbon, old rosary beads and a few dull centavos. With great care Filipa removed a tiny pouch which hung inside her shirt. Slowly, for her hands trembled, she pulled open its gathered neck and biting back her tears she removed a small wisp of baby hair. With meticulous care she separated three of the hairs from the lock and laid them at San Christóbal's feet.

She replaced the wisp in the pouch and tucked it all back under her collar. Settling her rebozo over her head, she clasped her hands to begin a prayer.

"Oh holy San Christóbal, who keeps our village safe," she began to whisper but stopped. Who does not keep our village safe, no, who allowed the terrible Utes to strike my husband dead and steal my only child—

She tried again.

"If you love us, if you have not forsaken us, for surely you have forsaken me, send me a sign. Let it be a real sign. If there remains in God's heart one tiny shred of concern for those He has abandoned, show me. Show me now. For I cannot bear one more day of this life and—"

Filipa's shoulders shook with sobs of pain and rage so that her voice rose beyond a prayerful murmur.

"If you do not answer, this is the last prayer I, Filipa, will ever make," she said and in her agony did not mind who heard. "If there is a God and if you are his Saint, then I beg you to strike Juan Vigil dead for who he is and what he has done. Amen!"

A few old parishioners lifted their heads from their devotions but only briefly. Pity the poor sorrowing woman, they thought. Pity us all.

It was only a remarkable coincidence, according to the priest who arrived in Las Trampas a few weeks later to say the burial prayers over the grave of Juan Vigil. But accidents happen all the time. Vigil had forced his horse chasing a sheep up a slippery slope. The beast had fallen, taken its rider several hundred feet down a cliff and landed on him. How the horse survived was truly a miracle.

When Filipa's neighbors spoke to the priest after the service, their faces showed no concern for Vigil, only for her. They said her anger was very great but her feeling of guilt was even greater. Because she truly believed that her prayer to San Christóbal had caused Vigil's accident, she had gone mad. She had taken to her bed and refused all nourishment. Convinced there was no way she could atone for her sin, she was determined to die and suffer in Hell for eternity. What a pity, the old priest agreed. She had once been so beautiful and happy. The death of a coward like Vigil ought not to torture her so.

The priest was an old man who had seen many things in his life. He had known Filipa since she was a young girl, tossing her long shining braid over her shoulder. But her natural pride was tempered with deep piety. He recalled the flowers she arranged on the altar when he came to Las Trampas and the delicious dishes she prepared for his dinners. He had blessed her marriage and he had baptized her children. He remembered pretty little María Guadalupe. The child would be now eight or so if his memory was correct. Yes, it was a great pity about the child. Surely she was dead and what a shame they could not bury her in the campo santo just above the church with her father. He would say a special prayer for her soul. Then he went to offer comfort to Filipa.

When he came to her house, the priest could see that she was near death. Too weak to rise, she received him lying on a blanket in the kitchen. Her dress was ragged, her hair was wild and matted. Her hands wrung a rosary as if they were strangling prayer.

Juan Vigil fell by accident, the old priest told her, not by San Christóbal's doing. The holy saint was too good, too close to God to even hear such a prayer. So she hadn't killed anyone.

Listening to the old priest's words, Filipa turned her face to the wall. "I have sinned, Father, don't deny me that truth," she whispered.

The priest sighed heavily. It was a mistake to persecute your own soul. Heaven knew there was enough real sin in the world. But he could see it would be useless to argue theology with her. She needed more than a lecture on church doctrine.

"While you are not guilty of actually causing Juan Vigil's death," he began, "you have sinned by wishing for it. The thought is father to the deed."

He could hear Filipa exhale.

"Yes, it is a very serious sin to even wish for the death of another human being," he continued, "and you must atone for it. Not for the death but to purify your heart."

Her thin hand moved unconsciously to cover that heart. The priest saw this and was pleased. However, the penance must be exactly right. He closed his eyes and said a little prayer to San Christóbal. Then his lips almost smiled.

"Yes, Filipa, you must atone for your mortal sin and the penance can not be an easy one." It was coming to him now. Filipa had turned her face to him and her eyes were large and bright as if with fever. Would the patient survive the cure?

"The life and death of Juan Vigil is irrelevant to you now," he said. "But for the sake of your immortal soul, which is of concern to God and to me, I order you to do a great penance. You will make a journey. And on this journey you will take all the sheep left by Juan Vigil and give them away to the poor."

The old man stretched his legs in front of him. His joints popped. He thought of how many miles he had travelled to serve God and wondered how many miles were left of his own journey.

"When you have given away all the sheep, your penance will be complete and your journey will be ended. Then your heart will be pure enough to understand God," he added. Goodness, what a prescription for a wounded soul. It was the strongest he had ever ordered. But he knew it was necessary.

"Will you promise to do this?" he asked gently.

Filipa nodded. When he made the sign of the cross, her hand unconsciously repeated the blessing. The priest promised to find her a dog to help.

She set out with Vigil's sheep and a skinny orphan pup. The village women had filled her sack with food. They hugged her thin shoulders and kissed her rough cheek, then watched as she started down the trail. It was a slow three days' walk with a flock to the next village.

The first night she slept in her cloak under a bush by the side of the road. Exhausted, she made no fire. But there was warm milk from a black ewe who had lost her lamb, enough for Filipa and the pup. In her dreams she saw the road stretch out before her, dark and rocky, endless, and the flock scattering into a bean field. In the dream she saw her husband's dog run circles fast and low to turn them, heard cries of the sheep like the

whimper of children in the night. Under the cries she heard a steady toc toc toc of hoofbeat going by. She woke feeling a hand was squeezing her heart. In the mist of sleep and dawn she thought she saw a dark figure on horseback vanish around a bend in the road.

The second day she spent gathering the straggling sheep but the pup was fast learning how to keep them together. That night again she shared the ewe's milk and her tortillas with the dog and slept in her cloak. The dream of the road returned and with it the sheep who tried to enter the bean field or turned back toward home, confused, milling among themselves with the same anxious cries. Under the poignant images she heard again the steady rhythm of hooves and when she woke, there was the smell of horse on the air as if someone had ridden past.

When she came to the tiny village of Córdova, she gave a sheep to a family whose husband and father had died of a coughing sickness. The townspeople fed her bread and beans. By evening she was out of Córdova. This night she made a small fire. Its heat felt good. The pup had worked the flock through the village very well, Filipa thought. The black ewe lay down nearby after milking. Filipa let herself watch the fire until it went out, grateful for the ewe's company.

At Pojoaque Filipa gave away two sheep, a ewe and its lamb, this time to a man raising five children alone. His wife had died in childbirth. At night the dream was the same, the road, the crying flock, their swift guardian and the sound of hooves.

Nambe, Tesuque, through Santa Fé to Agua Fría, down the long dusty road she drove the flock. In some villages no one was poor enough to accept a sheep. It did not matter to her. Nothing mattered, only the journey. She never thought of the end, she only travelled south.

Each night now, Filipa gathered sticks for her little fire. She warmed tortillas and beans on a stone and fed the dog. He was growing bigger and stronger every day. In a few weeks he had become a most useful shepherd. She did not like to think how much he reminded her of her husband's dog. He had the same soft face, the same way of cocking his head at her. His eyes reflected the fire as he watched over her.

The black ewe who gave such good milk attached herself to Filipa. When the sheep lay down quite close by, Filipa did not chase her away. Instead she rested her head on the ewe's soft fleece and slept. This time she dreamed of the days when she lived with her husband and Lupe. She was grinding the corn, the child was singing and her husband was stacking hay in the barn. He smiled lovingly at her. A warm flood of tears began to rise in Filipa and she pressed her face into the sweet wool. The ewe lay patiently under her sobs, breathing steadily, blinking her golden eyes in the firelight. Near dawn, Filipa woke to the fading hoofbeats.

Soon the black ewe would not leave her side. When she found herself walking close to the sheep, stroking her ears, Filipa knew she was becoming too fond of the creature. At Algodones, she gave the black ewe away. The sheep escaped and caught up with the flock the next day. In Bernalillo Filipa twice gave away the ewe but it was no use. The sheep came galloping after her, bleating piteously, thrusting her soft muzzle into Filipa's hand.

So she travelled the road south along the wild tossing river to Alameda, then through the outskirts of busy little Albuquerque village. Always people welcomed her into their homes as if she were their own. When her sandals wore out, they found another pair. When the rain was cold, they clothed her in warm woolen shawls. At first she would not accept their generosity. She was not trading the sheep, she tried to explain, she wanted nothing in return. But she soon saw their gifts were true expressions of love and concern, not barter. She then allowed herself to take what was offered and be grateful. It felt good to give thanks, warm like the fire.

The flock diminished as she gave one sheep to a very old man and a fat lamb to a band of luckless Indian hunters who were hungry. A young ram and two ewes went to a desperately poor family in Valencia whose livestock had all succumbed to a mysterious sickness. They took the three creatures and blessed her for them. Poor as Filipa was, she saw there were many who were poorer. Much as Filipa had suffered, she saw there were many who suffered even more.

Tomé, Belén, Vegita, La Joya and Chamizal, the villages slowly appeared and slowly receded behind her until the flock was reduced to two, just the black ewe and a big ram with beautiful horns she had saved, she realized, because the ewes had needed the comfort of his strength. But when these two last sheep were given away, she would return to Las Trampas. How far away it seemed. She had no idea how long she had been on the road, only that the days were shorter and the nights were very cold. Still, she was used to the sharp mountain air and in comparison the mild desert days seemed almost like summer.

Overhead the stars shimmered and twinkled. The same stars she had seen with wonder as a child and later—could she bear to remember those happy times—yes, later there were nights when she and her husband walked outside their warm

house just to look at the sky and marvel at its mysterious beauty.
Filipa missed his heavy masculine hand upon her shoulder, his
rough beard against her face.

And the infant Lupe, such a dear weight in her arms. She
had not allowed herself to think of Lupe since Juan Vigil had
died. Nor had she permitted herself to think of Vigil's death,
how it must have happened. Now she pictured the slippery
mud at the steep part of the slope. She could see Vigil's whip
fall on the horse's flank and the animal desperately scrambling,
the whip again and then the fall, the horse's legs in the air, the
man coming loose from the saddle as the horse rolled free of the
earth, the terrible smack of flesh on rock.

Vigil, killed by of his own miscalculation. She breathed
deeply as if she had been running. By his own miscalculation.

Poor Vigil, she thought, surprised at the idea. Poor Vigil.

Next to her the dog raised his head from his paws and lifted his ears. He was big now, well muscled, an excellent shepherd, so remarkably like her husband's dog. Perhaps sired by him, Filipa realized. The sheep who were lying by the fire with their legs folded neatly under them turned their big ears, too. Filipa strained to hear. Yes, on the wind, music, the sound of a flute. It faded and returned a little louder. How strange, she thought. Perhaps she was closer to Soccoro than she imagined. Yet there was no sign of the town, no tracks, no lights, no smoke. And the only travellers she had seen that day were headed north. A gust of wind blew the music towards her. Such a lovely sound, high and clear like someone singing. The dog rose to sniff the breeze and the sheep wrinkled their noses as if they smelled something they liked.

There had not been enough grass to satisfy them for the past three days. And they had not had water since morning. No doubt the animals smelled food, Filipa reasoned. But they would have to wait until they reached Soccoro tomorrow. Surely someone in that busy town would take them. Someone would water and feed them. Someone always has, Filipa thought as she pulled her cloak about her and let her head fall onto the ewe's side. She would miss her ewe and the handsome ram.

"Must I part with the dog, too?" she murmured into the delicate wool as she fell asleep. Tomorrow all would be resolved.

It was still dark when she woke. In the infinite blackness the music was even clearer. The sheep had left the glowing embers of the fire and the dog was standing on a rise not far off looking toward the sound. She would find the sheep in the morning. She closed her eyes again. What had she been dreaming? She returned to the image of her little house, the field green and thick with long heavy beans. And there was Lupe smiling at her, holding her apron full of corn. Lupe was singing and somehow the music of the flute was that sound. Under it all the hoofbeats faded.

Filipa opened her eyes to the early dawn sky. All was quiet. She would gather the last of her flock and enter Socorro before the sun rose. It seemed suddenly very important to be finished and return home.

The dog was at her side when she came to a little goat hut. Yes, there were her sheep foraging in the brush and behind the hut a horse grazed peacefully. The figure of a tall man stood by the door. Filipa could just make out his eyes, brilliant in the reflected campfire light. He raised his hand in greeting.

"I have come for my sheep," Filipa said. He nodded and handed her a bowl of broth.

"They were thirsty so I watered them," the man said in a soft low voice.

Filipa could not see any sign of water anywhere in the dry ground.

"And I had a little corn to spare," he added. "Enough for two hungry sheep."

"Thank you," Filipa replied. And then it occurred to her that she could give the sheep to this man and it would be over, the journey, her penance. Her heart lightened at the thought of returning to her own little house in Las Trampas.

"Would you like to have them?" she asked, sipping the delicious broth that warmed and renewed her insides.

But he shook his head and her heart sank.

"I thank you but I am not poor enough to accept your gift," he answered. "However I know someone much poorer than I. You must give the sheep to her." He gestured to the door of the hut. "I bought her for a lump of turquoise from a band of travelling Indians. She's in there."

Filipa peered inside. Asleep on a rude bed of hides was a beautiful young girl.

"Lupe!" she cried and embraced her daughter, dampening her hair with tears of joy. Yes, it was the darling of her heart, stolen by the Indians, who hugged her mother as if she would never let go. What a story she had to tell. The chief and his wife had so loved her singing, she said, they had treated her like a princess. And then this man had given them a huge turquoise stone and brought her here. She was thin but healthy and unmarked.

Outside the hut a golden sun was rising over the pink desert. The two sheep and the horse cast long morning shadows on the sandy plain. In the far west the Gallinas Mountains glowed purple in the sun's first rays. Filipa rose to thank the man who had rescued her daughter. The smoke of his camp fire rose gently into the fresh morning air. The saddled horse still grazed with the sheep but there was no sign of the man anywhere in the broad flat landscape.

Filipa called for him but no one answered. She sent the dog to find him but he returned without discovering anything. She stood watching for a long time but the man did not appear. The sun bathed her in its rosy glow. She felt light and clean, as if she had been scrubbed. She felt, she realized, happy, extremely happy. Whoever the stranger was, he had ended her journey. Her heart was full of gratitude.

She packed his belongings onto the horse and with her child, the sheep and the dog, headed into Soccoro to look for him there. But no one recalled ever seeing such a man, his horse, Lupe or even any travelling Indians.

In the little church on the plaza Filipa found a small bulto of San Christóbal. The carved figure of the Saint raised his right arm high in blessing. His face wore a most beatific smile. Filipa knelt before him and bowed her head. The thankful prayer came easily. When she had finished she removed the small pouch from her shirt, opened it and took out the precious wisp of hair. Digging deeper she found another lock of hair, this one thick and black, her husband's. She kissed them both and placed them at San Christóbal's feet.

She found the priest in the sacristy.

"What must I do with the horse and blankets?" Filipa asked after he had heard her story. He thought a moment, rubbing his chin. "You have a long road home," he advised. "Take the horse and the blankets. If such a man comes looking, I will tell him where to find you."

When Filipa and Lupe rode into Las Trampas with the sheep and the dog, the joyful village turned out to celebrate their return. It was nearly a year since Filipa had left on her journey and the little village looked very good to her. Everyone wanted to hear Lupe's stories about the Indians and what Filipa had seen in the wide world. Her faithful neighbors had planted her field and now young shoots poked up in the rows Vigil's sheep had destroyed the summer before. The lilacs were still blooming and her little house was warm and welcoming. Even the water in the acequia made its old sweet music.

In July the dog she named Christo would have his own little flock to mind for the black ewe would lamb. Later, Lupe would again grind her mother's corn and sing wedding songs. And when the old priest next came to Trampas, he would find Filipa's heart pure and pious, ready to receive God's blessing once again.

This happened a long time ago and there have been many, many offerings to San Christóbal ever since. The people of Las Trampas still hope that one day the mysterious stranger will arrive in search of his horse so they can thank him.

Truchas
Chile

Long black and purple clouds streaked a yellow sky as the sun sank into the western mountains. When the last animal was safely inside the corral, Elena shut the heavy gate behind her and struggled through the wiggling mass of creatures enclosed by four long walls of adjoining adobe houses. Every sheep, goat and cow was pushing to reach the evening hay the little boys had already forked into the center. She loved the solid, familiar bumping of the calves' bodies on hers and the goats' sharp smell. Dainty lips nibbled her fingers, horns brushed her legs as soft mud and manure underfoot sucked at the large boots she was wearing. Elena shuffled her feet to keep them from slipping off. They were her father's boots. He was not there to wear them himself because, like every Truchas man and boy over fourteen, he had been conscripted into the army to chase Navajos away from the pueblos along the Río Grande. How Papa hated to leave but Governor Mendinueta himself ordered every able-bodied man to defend the prosperous pueblos from raiding Indians. After all, it was the rich pueblo corn and cattle which fed the Governor's garrison, not pitiful chiles and beans from distant Truchas.

Elena ran her hands through the silky fur of a new cabrito whose baby horns were only nubs. Next spring the hair of this young goat would be long enough to shear, like the wool of the sheep. There were weavers in Chimayó who would buy it for their looms. One day Truchas would have surplus to trade in the markets. One day—but meantime, Elena was glad there was food to last through the winter. Until they cleared more land for planting, until they could cut more wood for lumber and fuel, until their strong men returned, they would have to get along as best they could with what they had.

Entering the house, Elena pulled off the boots, scraped them clean and set them carefully by the door. They stood alone against the wall because they were the only boots in the family. Just looking at their shape reminded Elena how Papa had hugged her when he left, telling her to take good care of her mother and the boys. Since she was the oldest of the three children, he had told her solemnly, she shared responsibility with her mother for keeping them all safe. Papa promised to be back for la Noche Buena, the most festive time of the year, and she was not too old to anticipate with joy the Christmas plays, the special Mass and days of feasting with which the pobladores of Truchas celebrated the birth of Jesus. But even the first snows of winter were a month away and there was still no word from him.

Elena loved this time of day when the chores were finished and the family ate together by the fire. And because she had worked to build it she was very proud of their house, a simple rectangular room divided by a curtain into sleeping and living areas. Above the heavy round pine ceiling vigas, tight rows of slender aspen trunks held the flat thick mud roof. Elena and her mother, Carmen, had mixed mud and straw for the adobes which dried in rectangular wooden forms under the hot summer sun. When the men had the adobe walls up and the roof on over the vigas, Elena and Carmen, with their neighbor women, mixed more mud and straw into a thick plaster which

they smoothed onto the adobe walls, inside and out, with their hands.

Elena looked around the house with pleasure and found nothing to improve on. When she married she would have one just like it. Two windows let a little sun in through the thick walls but were small enough to keep the warmth inside. In both corners of the long room bright fires in beehive-shaped kiva fireplaces snapped and popped a cheerful welcome. Elena inhaled the fragrance of her mother's posole stewing in a big iron pot. Posole with fresh pork, dried corn, onion, garlic and hot red chiles was a feast. Yes, there was a lot to be thankful for. Even without the men to help harvest, the crops had been bountiful that year. The weather was kind to both gardens and livestock. Apple trees bent nearly to the ground with fruit, squash fattened on the long vines, and now barrels of dried beans and chicos groaned with the plentiful supplies. Sacks of grain hung in the corners of every house. This year there was even a little wine from their own vines fermenting in two clay jars standing against the wall. Braids of gourds, garlic and onions hung outside the house walls on the viga ends. But most colorful were the long ristras of fiery red chiles hanging in fat clusters. Fresh or dried, hot chile peppers flavored almost every dish the mountain women prepared.

They had slaughtered two big pigs that week so there was plenty of tender pork for everyone's stewpot. The pigs' hides were nailed to frames. For the next several days Elena and the other girls old enough to work but too young to have families of their own would rub hog fat and brains into the hides to soften and preserve them. When traders came through they could exchange these cured hides, their extra ground corn meal and beans for guns and powder. If the traders had any guns, which were rare in the colony. Even the governor complained he had no guns for his soldiers because the Spanish Crown would not bother to arm its northern territory where there was no gold. And raiding Indians stole every gun they could get their hands on. They used them to hunt, of course, but they also used them against the pobladores who, they said, had stolen their land.

"Why don't they grow their own food instead of taking ours," Elena asked. But no one had the answer to a question like this. Sometimes Indians came peacefully to trade, sometimes they came like a murderous horde. Like the weather, there was nothing the people of Truchas could do about them. Especially without guns.

All summer the village had talked of nothing but the July raid. It occurred right after Papa's troop reluctantly left for the garrison. One morning, a band of Comanches quietly appeared out of the forest, locked everyone into one house and ransacked the village. First they packed all the dry food they could find into sacks. Then they ate all the cooked food they could get their hands on, right out of the pots. Elena's tamales, Carmen's tortillas, a smoked cabrito vanished. A very tall Indian poured a pan of flan down his throat, dripping the custard and its precious sugary juices onto his bare chest. To Elena's disgust, he then licked the pan and flung it into the bushes. A dog had better manners, she thought. After they had

eaten every scrap of food, they pawed through Carmen's chest
of linens and turned over the mattress looking for money and
jewels. They had no respect for anything, Elena could see that.
They even pulled the nests out from under her broody hens. It
had taken Elena days to collect the terrified chickens and then
they didn't lay any eggs for a month afterward.

An Indian boy not much older than her brothers held their
spotted horses while the men gathered the two fattest sheep and
tied them, helpless and bleating, onto the backs of their ponies.
One was Elena's's own ewe, an orphan she had raised by the
hearth, one she loved like a pet and counted on to give her
lambs for many years. Upon hearing the ewe's pitiful cries,
Elena wept for she knew Comanche warriors did not raise
sheep, they only ate them.

Burdened with as much loot as the horses could carry, the
Indians finally departed, leaving the village a shambles. It took

the strongest women half an hour to batter open the stoutly locked shutters so a child could squeeze through to unlock the door. After the village counted up their losses, they gathered to offer a prayer of thanksgiving that the Indians had at least spared their lives.

But these prayers of gratitude were meager offerings. Every single person in Truchas knew there was nothing to prevent the Indians from returning to pluck them clean when the harvest was in and there would not be a man back from army duty to defend them.

A few suggested they abandon Truchas and return to Santa Fé where they would be safe. But they had left that town where they lived in cold, miserable huts, diseased and hungry when the Governor granted them this land to farm. Because he had encouraged them to settle in the high lands, he would not leave them unprotected. As soon as he knew the Comanche were coming in from the east, he would send their men home. And he would send guns.

Besides, the deep snows of winter would keep Indians away. If they could just hold out until the ground was well covered, they would be safe. After long days and nights of talk, the village determined that they would stay. They could not leave the houses they had built with their own hands, the fences they had made from timber they had cut themselves nor the land they had cleared and planted with such hope. On their own farms, poor as they were and harsh as the seasons might be, once and for all they were masters of their lives. They would not give that up, they would defend it, somehow. It was all they thought about during the summer and into fall.

After supper, Elena took buckets out to the spring to fetch water for the boys' weekly bath. If there was enough yucca soap left over she might wash her hair. It took a long time to dry by the fire but she and her mother could work on the quilt they were making out of rags. She dipped the buckets into the spring and set them on the sandy ground, then paused to smell the sweet piñon smoke from the chimneys. The interiors of all the little houses were bright with cooking fires. The wind sighed through twisted junipers under an immense sky. Elena looked up. There were so many stars, many more than anyone in Santa Fé could possibly see. She was forgetting what that town had been like, letting it go. This was her land, her sky, as much a part of her as her eyes and hands. No, Papa would say they were right to stay, in spite of the danger. The village had lived through the July raid, they would make it through another. At least they had prepared themselves as best they could. Maybe God had heard their prayers and sent the Comanches somewhere else.

An owl hooted softly. Elena turned her face to the sound. When another hooted a short distance from the first, the hair on the back of Elena's neck stood up. Listening carefully she heard the faint click of a hoof striking a pebble which made a small hissing noise as it rolled into the arroyo. Someone or something was very close to her, observing her. She emptied the buckets onto the ground and hurried into the house.

"They're here, Mama," she whispered urgently. Carmen paused for only a moment at the fire, quickly put down the long spoon and crossed herself. The little boys who had been wrestling on the bed sat up and put on their coats without a word. They all hugged each other and then the boys hurried silently outside, one to the left neighbors, one to the right, to pass the warning. In a few minutes, there was the sound of buckets emptying out back doors and then everything was still. One by one the candles went out until only firelight illuminated the rooms. Even the village dogs which had begun to bark were silenced. Only the animals in the corral milled nervously.

When the Indians appeared no one screamed with terror, no one dashed out into the night, no one even seemed surprised. Except for the crying babies and cranky children awakened from sleep, there was hardly any fuss at all when the band of painted men peered into the cozy rooms from whose hearths such delicious smells emanated. It was the same

Comanche band. They herded all the villagers into the same house where they had been held captive before. Hiding their nervousness, everyone quietly obeyed. Almost everyone, that is, except Elena, her brothers and three other boys who had hidden themselves among the animals in the corral, according to the plan.

Taking a cautious peek through the window, Elena watched as the Comanche men stretched their weary bodies and investigated their small house. The one who seemed to be the chief put a spoon into Carmen's posole, nodded approvingly and invited the others to join him. They all smacked their lips appreciatively at the plump kernels of corn in the steaming broth and blew on dripping pork ribs to cool them.

When they had emptied the pot, the chief sent his men to bring food from the neighbors' houses. Soon the table was crowded with fragrant beans and pans of corn biscuits, casseroles of meaty enchiladas and crispy brown chunks of roasted pork. Scooping the dripping stews with tortillas into their wide mouths, tossing the bones onto the floor, the Indians devoured every single tamale and burrito, every biscochito and pudding, right down to the last crumb, When they had finished eating they leaned back against the wall by the fires or stretched out among the debris of their feast, burping and rubbing their stomachs with satisfied, sleepy expressions.

It was not until one accidentally hit his head on a jar that they discovered the wine. With howls of delight the Comanches dipped bowls into the fermenting alcohol and drank it up as if it were only water. They finished one olla and opened the other. They were soon tipsily singing and even dancing, tripping over the sleeping bodies of their comrades. When they knocked the crucifix and several strings of garlic off the wall, they laughed uproariously. While they argued over who should finish the wine, Elena signalled her brothers to follow her.

Like shadows they slipped through the corral gate, hugged the dark side of the building and peered around the corner.

There sat the lad who was guarding the horses, younger than
Elena, she guessed from his size. Probably his father was one of
the men making a hog of himself in her house. Good, eat like
a pig and sleep it off. She sucked in her breath disapprovingly.
Like his father, the boy probably thought Truchas was an easy
mark without its menfolk. Drop in for dinner, destroy everything and help yourself to our animals, knowing full well we
can't fire a shot and there isn't a man within twenty miles to
help. The memory of her dear, helpless ewe trussed to the back
of an Indian horse was as vivid as ever. You act as if you're enti-
tled to everything, Elena thought. This time it isn't going to be
so easy.

She unfolded a length of white linen her mother was saving
for her wedding dress and threw it over her head. Hidden in the
bend of the arroyo she circled the spring. The Indian boy guarding the horses sat with his back against a fence post, watching
the older men feast. A horse snorted when he caught Elena's
scent but the boy did not turn his head. He's probably tired,
Elena thought. The men haven't brought him any food so he's

probably hungry, too. When she was only ten feet from the boy she raised her white robed arms. The linen fluttered in the evening wind like the feathers of a strange bird. This time all the horses lifted their heads and blew their noses fearfully. As the boy looked around to see what was causing the disturbance, Elena stood up with her shrouded arms outstretched and approached the boy, howling. He rose and made an attempt to run but stumbled and then stood rooted to the ground.

"Yes, I am a witch!" Elena hissed. Whether or not he understood her Spanish, he clearly knew about witches. Like a ghost she glided towards him and when she was close enough, she flung a handful of hot chile powder into his wide eyes. The boys jumped him from behind, gagged and trussed him, then dragged his bound body into the arroyo and stood watch over him. It was done in less than two minutes. Not one Comanche appeared to have heard anything of the tussle, Elena noted. They weren't bothering to post a real look-out because they thought they were in no danger from mere women and children. In fact, the drunken singing in Elena's house was now mostly snoring. A man staggered out to the darkness and vomited, holding the branches of a juniper for support. A second unsteadily emerged to take wood from the stack by the door to add to the fire. Then they went back inside, throwing the door shut behind them.

Elena left the linen shroud on a branch and with her brothers, crept back up the arroyo. When they came to the houses, one boy climbed a wooden ladder to the long, flat roof where many fruits and vegetables were laid out to dry. The other slipped back through the gate into the corral among the animals. Flattened to the walls, Elena stealthily made her way to the front window of her house where snoring noises rose and fell in uneven waves. She wrinkled her nose. The smell of vomit and unwashed men disgusted her. How could their wives stand them? Yet, asleep, they snored like her father and his brothers. It was just barely possible they were some kind of human beings under their paint and feathers. If they cleaned up and behaved themselves, possibly—then her eye caught the sight of her father's boot. One of them was wearing it, yes, she could see he had both of them on. How could he! No, they were not human beings, they were bárbaros, savage raiders who had stolen her ewe and they might even carry her off, make her a slave wife and she would never see her dear father again. Papa's boots! They weren't going to get away with it.

Elena took a deep breath and tried to clear her mind. Right now the important thing was to follow the plan. It had been her idea from the start and she had finally persuaded her mother and the others that it was the best and only defense Truchas could muster. But as Elena stood so near the window, so near the sleeping Indians inside, doubt paralyzed her. What was it Papa had said? You're a big girl now, I'm counting on you, that was it. Then, take good care of your mother. Elena's thoughts swam. If Papa thought she could take care of Mama, she could. Fragments of Christmas memories shot through her mind. Midnight mass, the supper after, laughter. It would be Buena Noche again and Papa would be there. She could almost feel his strong hand around her shoulder. Nobody makes chile stew like my Elena, he always said. Nobody's smarter than my Elena, not even Indians, he would say this year. Though her knees were knocking and her heart was beating wildly, she would not run. She would make the plan work. Her fluttering heart steadied.

She looked up to find her brother peering down at her over the edge of the roof. She nodded and pointed at the windows. He nodded, then turned away. Slowly and silently her trembling hand closed the heavy wooden shutters on the two small windows. The hinges made no noise because she had greased them lavishly with pig fat that morning as she had every morning for the past month. Slowly and silently she locked the heavy bolts holding the shutters closed. She pressed the thick oak door tight against its frame and gently, oh so gently, eased the mighty iron bar across and secured it. She listened over the pounding of the blood in her head but the Indians made no sign they had heard anything. The snoring only intensified.

In a moment, her brother reappeared, raised his thumb to signal that the back windows and door were secure. He grinned. How white his teeth looked against his dark face. Then he was busy at the chimneys, yes, pouring chile powder down the smoky openings onto the fires below. A whole sack in each one to start and more if necessary, that was the plan. Elena leaned against the rough adobe wall and heaved a deep, shaky sigh. It was happening, there was no turning back. She prayed the plan would work, it had to work. As she went to release her mother and the others from their imprisonment, she heard the hollow clunk of heavy boards over the chimney holes. Oh what a blessing to have such clever, steady little brothers, she thought. Thanks to them the plan was operating right on schedule. In a few minutes burning chile would take its effect.

The women and children waited nervously in a little knot outside Elena's house. At first there was just a little coughing from one Indian but it soon grew to loud hacking from several. They were awake now. When they found they could not open the oak door or the shutters they began to shout angrily. But the angrier they got, the more their coughing became mixed with gagging and choking and even strangling noises. Elena cringed and hugged her mother as the sounds grew more desperate. There was the protesting squawk of the heavy plank table being drawn across the floor, then an awful battering on the sturdy oak door. The door held but Elena shuddered, thinking of the disorder of their tidy house. Crockery smashed and the smell of vomit hung in the pure night air. Oh Mary, Mother of God, a woman moaned and fell to her knees to pray.

One Indian tried to beat the window shutters open with a cook pot, she could tell by the ringing the iron made. But the strong bolts held and soon the trapped men were choking too hard to beat on anything. One was speaking in broken Spanish. His comrades were dying, he yelled. He begged the villagers to open up. But the Truchas plan called for a tough stance. The Truchas people would open the door only if certain conditions were met, many voices called back.

There was some low talk among the coughing while the Comanches considered this. Then, the sound of arguing voices and the smashing of a big piece, probably a wine olla. Perhaps they were looking for something with which to put the fires out. Of course there was no water in any of the houses, the house-holders had seen to that. The choking began anew and the now very enfeebled Indians agreed to hear what they wanted.

Elena pushed Carmen forward. Her mother hadn't wanted to be the speaker but her husband had been elected alcalde, not that Truchas had a real mayor, and it was Elena's idea. Besides, there was no one else to do it. Carmen cleared her throat but her voice sounded thin and feeble anyway.

The pobladores of Truchas would let them out alive, she said, but only if the chief gave his word that he would leave them in peace. In peace now and forever! The little group surrounding her chorused their support of this and patted Carmen on the back. Go on, they urged, tell them the rest. Finish them, do it now. From within the smoking house, there were immediate cries of compliance mixed with retching and piti-ful groans though no one could have said for certain if it was due entirely to the deadly chile fumes or the powerful wine the Indians had drunk.

Encouraged by this, Carmen called in a stronger voice that they must leave all their guns and ammunition behind. This demand was met by silence, a few muffled coughs and renewed banging on the door. But quick as a wink the two boys on the roof were tipping powdered chile into the chimneys again. The little group below drew their rebozos more closely around them and prepared to wait, confident now in the effectiveness of the smoke. Had they not planted, harvested, dried and ground the fieriest seeds from the fieriest plants? Was there a child in the village who had not been threatened with the dreaded chile

punishment for talking back or forgetting to close a gate? Not
that a Truchas parent would actually inflict such harm on any
child. However, the threat was a sharp goad to improved be-
havior.

So they stood and waited for the fumes to do their awful
work. Enough chile smoke could stop even a strong human
heart. They waited and they listened. Amid the desperate gasps
for air there was a hoarse croak of agreement from the spokes-
man. The men, he said, would give up their guns in exchange
for their lives.

Carmen looked around her nervously but Elena held her
arm firmly. They mustn't quit until they had everything they
deserved. Carmen cleared her throat and spoke. The Comanches must not only promise never to return and leave all their
guns, they must also leave three good horses to pay for the
animals and food they had stolen in the summer. Inside there
was silence, then groans of agreement. The village people nod-

ded and made approving sounds among themselves for the plan was working just as they hoped.

Now, Carmen said, they must throw the guns out the window first. The Comanche should know that one of their own sons was captive. After a brief silence, they agreed. When Elena opened the shutter the tiny window was jammed with tear-streaked Indian faces dragging fresh air into their lungs. Then four long guns hit the ground and several little sacks of powder and shot. The children quickly stacked the muskets against the wall. When Elena's brother slid open the door bolt, one by one the bent, weakened figures of the once formidable Comanche men filed through with their hands over their faces. Like bad boys who've been punished, Elena thought. It was a fine sight and she tried to capture every detail to tell her father. First the tall one who had eaten the flan in July, his face red and his nose streaming, then the one who took her ewe, eyes swollen shut, blindly feeling his way out. Then the chief, a young man, slim and muscular, and then—the one wearing Papa's boots appeared! It was too much to bear.

"Give me my father's boots," she screamed. She grabbed a gun from the wall, pointed it at the Indian and fired. The gun's recoil threw her onto her back but the target himself was unharmed, though blackened by the exploding powder. Either the gun had misfired or her aim with the heavy weapon was poor. But that made no difference to Elena who clambered to her feet, seized a rock and plunged screaming through restraining arms to beat the thief. But of course a girl is no match for a man. The offending Comanche pinned her arms as if she were a straw doll and turned in mute appeal to his chief. However, the sight of Elena in the hands of a Comanche so infuriated the mothers and children of Truchas that for many long moments the peaceful stars over New Mexico looked down upon women and children attacking ferocious Indian warriors with nothing more than their bare hands.

"Enough," the chief cried in Spanish, lifting up his arms for order. "Peace now, everyone!" he cried more loudly. His voice had a sobering effect for in a moment the yelling and scratching and kicking was over. Then the chief said something to the Indian which made him remove the boots and hand them to Elena. She jerked them from his hands, thinking how good it would feel to slap his face. But her mother pulled her back, insisting, enough, that's enough now.

When all had quieted, the chief surveyed the people who stood before their houses. A few doddering old folks, several young children and their mothers but not a single gun, not even a man to use it among them, they stood totally helpless against the force of his weapons and the hardened intentions of his warriors. And yet the village, it could be said, had defeated him. Or had the Comanches defeated themselves? The chief's black hair gleamed in the starlight, his beaded trousers sparkled. His high-bridged nose still streamed and his eyes were red from the chile. "Peace," he repeated, sounding tired. "Quiet now."

"Hermanas y niños," he continued and the trace of a smile appeared on his face when his eyes found Elena, still flushed with anger and victory. Who are you calling sisters and children, she muttered but her mother hushed her. As the chief spoke, everyone fell into respectful silence. There was something in his eyes that held them, a fierce pride, perhaps a desperate pride, Elena thought. "I give you my word that as long as I, Cuerna Verde, am chief no Comanche will come to your village again," he said. "Not because you might have killed us, although you could have. We do not fear death nor do we expect mercy. No, we leave you in peace because you are a brave people like us. Your husbands and fathers have good reason to be proud of such strong wives and children." Elena could not help but admire the power and dignity of his graceful posture, his clear and certain speech. Speaking proper Spanish, he sounded as if he might be a human being after all. Perhaps such people had wives and children, a life not unlike what she knew. A low murmur of grudging approval rose and fell among the pobladores and the Indian boy was released. A Comanche tied three strong horses to the corral rails. The chief and his men mounted the rest of their horses, some riding double.

"Tell your husbands when they return from the Governor's army that we admire the courage and cunning of their women," the chief said. He wheeled his horse away, then back for a final word. "And tell them their wives are excellent cooks." Now there was a distinct smile on his handsome face. He turned his horse again toward the mountain, raised his hand as if to say good-bye, then led his band into the night.

And that is how chile saved Truchas. The husbands and fathers did return to their village in time for Christmas. To their great joy they found their women and children not only safe and healthy, but in good spirits, for chief Cuerna Verde, the most ferocious and respected of all the Comanches—who would one day die by a Spanish sword—was true to his word and left the village undisturbed. Elena's great, great grandchildren say there was quite a fiesta on that Buena Noche and for years to come. You may be sure they celebrated with plenty of chile, especially Elena's own extra hot and smoky "Posole Comanchero". And they are eating it still.

Arcia
and the
Fallen Star

Arcia let the cold water run over the translucent membranes to rinse away the half-digested grasses and leaves. In the babble of the river's edge, she could hear voices but not what they were saying. Probably the voices of the river were saying she was stupid and clumsy, that's what her sisters always said. But they weren't her sisters, they were her father's step-children and they were older and taller and they didn't like her. They hadn't liked her since she came to live with them. How sad she felt sometimes, ever since Mama died. But it was no use wishing for things to be the way they once were, they kept telling her. She hated being such a crybaby in front of them. She knew she was getting too old for it. But when they were mean to her she just couldn't help feeling sorry for herself. Arcia wanted to be strong. Ignore what they say, be brave, grow up, she told herself. But she didn't feel brave or grown up.

She stretched open the delicate, blue-veined tubes of sheep intestine and let them float gently on the surface of the rippling water. They would make good strong casings for sausage. She would grind meat and seasonings together, then stuff it into the membranes and hang them to dry in the smoke of the kitchen fire. Papa loved her sausage best but the others just ate it as if it were straw. Rosa, her father's wife, was always praising the food her own Angelina and Belinda made as if it were a miracle they could roll a simple tortilla but she never said anything nice about Arcia's cooking.

Her hands were numb from the cold water. She turned to spread the clean cloth on which she would lay the casings. How yellow the cottonwoods had become. The last leaves clung to their branches and carpeted the ground below the old trees with gold. And the chamisa bushes, a paler shade of yellow, looked so pretty beside the tall purple asters and low, dark blue verbena. September was such a lovely time of the year. There was a splash behind her. She turned but not quickly enough to reach the sausage casings which were dangling from the claws of a red tailed hawk. His broad, powerful wings lifted him into the air and away from her. With a shrill scream he disappeared over the trees.

Arcia's mouth hung open for several long seconds. Why did that bird steal her food when he could hunt for himself! And why pick on her? Now there would be no special treat for her father when he came home next month. Her throat thickened with the old familiar tears. She knew what they would say when she got back to the house. Look, Mama, Arcia's feeding the birds our food. We're starving while she throws good tripas down the river. She's useless, a daydreamer.

Hot tears burned her cheeks. Deep sobs shook her body, then subsided. She had to face it, crying wouldn't bring anything back. She stood and folded the empty white cloth. The golden leaves of the cottonwoods were still beautiful, that was something. And the red feathers of the hawk, his curved beak and big yellow talons were so pretty. She had never seen a red tail so close before. She sniffled back the last tears. What, he was flying over the river again right towards her. Did he think she had more food for him? He circled over her head, very close, too close. She dropped to her knees and tried to wave him away. She could feel the wind of his wings on her hair, she could feel his feathers just touch her face and then he was gone. He hadn't hurt her, hadn't scratched her with those claws, thank goodness. She stood up and wiped her face with her hands. There was something stuck onto her forehead, a stone or some grit, a little piece of sand, perhaps. Arcia rubbed but whatever it was would not come off. She dipped the cloth in the river and rubbed until it hurt but the stone or metal spot was there to stay.

She washed her hands and arms again and dusted off her clothes. It was still there. Perhaps a stone had somehow lodged in her skin. At least it wasn't painful. She would look in the mirror when she got home.

Later, when the sun was directly overhead and her little yellow cat rubbed its head on her leg then settled happily into her lap, Arcia sat in the barn doorway and peered into the mirror.

The silver paint was coming off the back and the glass itself was cracked right down the middle. Still, it was better than nothing. Arcia turned her face so the rays of sunlight fell on her forehead. Whatever the thing in her skin was, it was bright and yellow. She rubbed it with a finger. It was about an inch wide, flat, and it had pointy edges. And it was not coming off, no matter how she picked at it.

"Arcia!" Rosa was calling her. "What are you doing! Take this bucket to the pigs and harness the pony. We're going to market today. Arcia!"

She put down the mirror and hurried into the house. The kitchen was a mess but she could clean up while they were gone. She took the bucket of leftovers out to the pigs and while they greedily gobbled it up, she scratched their rough backs. The chickens pecked hopefully around her feet and the rooster stretched his beautiful neck and crowed proudly at her. How agreeable animals were compared to people.

She brushed the pony and fastened his harness to the cart as Rosa and her daughters came out the door, warmly dressed in thick wool capes and fur muffs. Rosa always said it would be a waste of good clothes to dress Arcia like Angelina or Belinda since she was only mucking out the barn, giving hay to the animals or up to her elbows in wash water. Besides, Rosa declared, her girls had always been delicate. Arcia was more suited to work because her mother had been just a farmer. Instead of pretending to shiver in the cold, Arcia should be grateful that she had the opportunity to live with Rosa and her two well-bred daughters. It would elevate her mind to know such refined girls.

Arcia stood by the pony's head while they got into the cart.

"The whip!" Rosa cried impatiently. "You know I must have the whip to get the pony up the hill!" Arcia shrugged her shoulders and looked at the ground.

"I can't find it," she said. She had cut it up and thrown it in the river. Rosa's mouth tightened and her daughters' faces looked exasperated.

"You couldn't find your own nose," the girls chimed together. They made ugly faces at Arcia.

"After all I've done for you, you are the most useless clod on the face of this earth. First you're feeding the birds with food off our own table," Rosa said, reminding Arcia of the scolding she had endured earlier. "And now you've lost a valuable piece of equipment. What am I to do with you?" Arcia trembled but she pretended she didn't even hear what Rosa was saying. Let them get out and walk instead of using the whip, she thought but she kept a humble expression on her face. It worked, this time her tears didn't humiliate her.

"Are you sure she's hooked everything up right," the older girls whined at their mother, peering at the harness from their comfortable seats. Rosa ignored this. How would any of them know whether the harness was properly fastened? Then the glittering thing above Arcia's eyes caught her attention.

"Arcia, come here, come closer this very minute," she said sharply. "What's that on your forehead? Take it off right now and show me." Angelina and Belinda immediately leaned forward to see what it was that Arcia was now hiding under her hand.

"Nothing, really, it's nothing," Arcia mumbled. "Some dirt or something." But they were all squinting at her. Obediently, she moved closer.

"Take your hand down, don't try to hide anything from us," Rosa said. The three of them examined Arcia's face intently.

"It's a star!" Angelina said.

"It's a gold star," Belinda added, touching it with a finger. She tried to pick it off.

"Ouch!" Arcia cried, stepping back. "Don't, it doesn't come off, I tried."

"Where did you get this," Rosa demanded. "How did it get onto your forehead! I'm your mother now, don't try to keep any secrets from me!" She sounded angry.

She is not my mother, Arcia thought, and she never will be.

But she kept this to herself and told them how the hawk who had stolen the sausage casings had flown back over her and dropped the star onto her forehead.

"Almost as if he were thanking her for the meal," Angelina cried.

"Yes, he was showing her his gratitude for our food," Belinda added. Rosa was observing Arcia closely. She lifted the girl's chin and turned her face first one way then the other. She turned Arcia by the shoulders and looked her up and down. Then she looked at her own daughters. Angelina was quite plump for her age and her front teeth had big spaces between them. Belinda's teeth were good but there were spots on her face and her rather large ears stuck out no matter how she fixed her hair. Belinda had also inherited her mother's unfortunately long nose and tiny eyes.

Rosa sighed. She had never looked closely at Arcia before, she hadn't bothered. Arcia was usually splattered with mud and her hair hung down and stuck to her sweating face. But the star gleaming on the girl's forehead made her take a good look and Rosa didn't like what she saw. Arcia had clear brown eyes fringed with thick lashes, unblemished rosy cheeks, and luxuriant hair, almost black with rich red tints, so unlike Angelina's pale strands that made only one skinny braid. It was quite a graceful body under the short, lumpy dress, a hand-me-down from Belinda. Surely Arcia had not been this—she could hardly bear to think of the word but there it was—*pretty* all along. Surely in the past three years she would have noticed the slender neck, the gently swelling bosom, the strong well-shaped hands. Arcia had changed overnight, no, that very morning. And only one thing could explain the change, the star on her forehead. It was a sign that she was favored, destined to be a beauty with all the advantages beauty commanded: the admiration of rich, powerful men, marriage into privilege, wealth and security. Neither of her own daughters were likely to achieve these lofty goals. And where did that leave her? The

mother of undowried girls who might never find husbands. Rosa bit her lip in frustration. It wasn't fair! Sure, they were bickering nasty girls—Rosa stifled this criticism of her darlings. No no no, they were every bit as good as Arcia. If they wore the star, they would become instantly beautiful just the way Arcia had.

"Unhitch the pony, Arcia." She would not tolerate the discrepancy one minute more. "Angelina! Belinda! Get down. Go inside, change your clothes. No, wait, don't change your clothes, just come with me!" There was no time to lose. The hawk might be flying off that minute to bestow stars on other girls.

Arcia watched as the mother and her two daughters stumped down to the river bearing strips of fresh meat for the hawk. They stood and called to the bird but the sky remained empty. Finally Rosa returned with Belinda and their faces were gloomy.

"Finish the chores," they said to Arcia, then went inside and closed the door. Angelina had stopped waving the dripping meat and was strolling aimlessly under the cottonwoods when the hawk appeared over the hill and circled. She ran out into the open, arms wide, thrusting her offering to the heavens when the bird swooped down, just as he had over Arcia, and brushed her with his wings. He took the meat in his talons but dropped it into the river. Angelina shrieked with joy, feeling her forehead.

"I can feel it! It's there, I know it's a star and it's even bigger than Arcia's," she cried, running up to the house. The door flew open as her mother and sister ran to rejoice with her.

But it was not a star on Angelina's forehead. It was a small green horn a little bigger than a mole. Rosa gasped and stood back. Thank heaven it was near the hairline, not that there was enough hair on her daughter's head to cover it. Perhaps it was only temporary. Could a hat disguise it? Glaring at Arcia as if it were her fault, she hustled the daughters inside. There was a clattering of pans in the kitchen and loud protests from Angelina, then howls of pain but it wasn't until supper that night that Arcia learned the cause of the commotion. Angelina's forehead wore a bulging bandage and her face a furious expression.

"Oh, don't blame me, I was only trying to remove it," Rosa remarked angrily to her daughter. "You're the one who wanted a gold star." Their eyes turned on Arcia who was serving them. The ragged dress she wore seemed as fine as chiffon. Her hair glowed in the firelight and her slender waist, cinched in by an old leather thong, was no bigger than Belinda's ankle. Yes, Arcia was becoming almost beautiful, Rosa thought. The idea irritated her no end.

"Sit up straight or you'll get a hump," she snapped at Angelina who glowered back at her mother and rounded her shoulders defiantly until her nose was nearly in the soup.

"I would never act that way towards my mother," Arcia thought to herself. But then, if her mother had spoken to her like that, maybe she would. For the first time, Arcia felt sorry for Angelina.

"Can I get you a compress?" she asked.

"You can get lost, is what you can do," Angelina replied.

"Yes, mind your own business," Rosa added.

"Who asked you?" Belinda chimed in.

There were loud arguments among the three all night and the next morning.

"Maybe Angelina didn't deserve a gold star but I do and I'm going to get it!" Belinda screamed as she slammed out of the house. She carried a dripping hunk of flesh to the river and called the hawk to come to her. But as on the day before, the sky remained clear. Not a swallow flew anywhere near the river or the house. By noon Arcia had fed the pigs and chickens and milked the cow. She had turned the sheep and goats out to pasture and churned the milk. The breakfast dishes were done and a great pot of posole was bubbling on the kitchen fire. The barn was swept and firewood was chopped and stacked neatly by the door. Her little yellow cat was winding itself around her feet as Arcia gathered soiled laundry to boil in the yard when she saw the hawk come over the hill. He circled Belinda who had lain down under the trees for a nap. The hawk landed on a branch and squawked. Belinda opened her eyes and jumped up, holding the meat out in front of her.

"Nice hawk," she called. "Nice birdie! Give me a star like Arcia's. Only bigger!" The hawk flew in circles around her.

"I don't want a horn on my forehead," Belinda shrieked as the hawk swooped low, brushing her with its wings. This time it didn't bother to take the meat but just flew on. As it passed by Arcia the hawk gave a little scream and disappeared over the hills. Then Belinda was running up to the house, wailing and crying that she had nothing, nothing at all on her forehead.

"Damned bird," she sobbed, "he could have scratched my eyes out! After I offered him that good meat." Her mother and sister had rushed out to examine her but there was nothing at all on her forehead.

"At least I didn't get a horn like stupid Angelina," she said, sticking her tongue out at her furious sister. Her mother was telling her she could try again, perhaps the next day, perhaps that very afternoon. She patted Belinda's stout shoulder and then gave a little cry, followed by a really big scream of horror.

"What's the matter," Belinda shrieked. Rosa pointed at her ear. When Angelina saw it, she screamed, too. Then she laughed. Arcia hurried over to look and gasped. Belinda was feeling her ears which had become hairy and grown several inches long, like a donkey's. They were even twitching back and forth. Poor, unfortunate Belinda, Arcia thought, reaching out a hand to touch them, thinking of how they might be concealed.

"Don't touch me! Get away, you witch!" Belinda shrieked, slapping Arcia's hand down.

"Yes, get away from us. It's all your fault," the three yelled together. Rosa put her arms around Belinda as far as they would reach to comfort her.

"Poor baby, look what Arcia has done to you," she murmured, then glanced at her daughter's new ears and shuddered.

"What about me? I guess you don't care that I have a big green horn growing out of my head which is much, much worse," Angelina wailed. She was so beside herself she danced in little circles and beat her fists on her sides. The she tore off her bandage and stamped on it. Rosa took one look and burst into tears for the little horn was a bit larger than before the operation. For several long minutes the peaceful air was rent with sorrow and despair. But when Arcia brought them handkerchiefs to blow their noses, they thrust her aside. And when she offered to make tea, they turned on her.

"You're the cause of all our misery," Angelina hissed.

"Don't even try to touch the hem of my dress," Belinda snarled.

"Why don't you go live in the barn with all those animals you are so fond of," Rosa barked. "There's plenty of room for you and the cat to sleep in the hay!"

"Oh dear," Arcia thought as she returned to her chores. "What are these changes going on in us?" For there were changes going on inside Arcia, too. Not only did she feel sorry for Angelina but now she pitied Belinda and even Rosa. Such unhappy people! It was much easier to sleep in hay than to wear donkey ears or a horn on your forehead.

As for the star, Arcia wondered why they made so much fuss over it. Nothing wonderful had happened to her life. Quite the contrary, they disliked her more than ever. The one small improvement was she had stopped feeling sorry for herself. But that had nothing to do with a piece of metal in her skin. Or did it? At any rate Arcia was awfully glad she didn't have a horn or those terrible ears. No one deserved that. She had begun to think about her stepsisters a little differently since the star fell onto her forehead. They never said anything nice to her but they never said anything nice to each other, either. They were almost as mean to each other as they were to her. No wonder they were so unhappy. She wished she could do something to make them feel better but everything she tried just made them angrier.

As September passed into October, neither Angelina's horn nor Belinda's donkey ears went away but seemed to grow a little larger. Although her daughters complained that their new bonnets chafed, Rosa insisted they wear them all day, in case someone should stop by and see them. None of them spoke to Arcia except to tell her what to do. Although Rosa forbade them to even look at themselves in the mirror, every day they examined themselves and every day each told the other she was uglier than before. All of them blamed Arcia for it.

By mid-October Arcia had gathered the apples to dry and shocked corn stalks in the field for the cow to eat when snow came. She had mended all their winter clothes and knitted new mittens and hats for everyone. She could hardly wait for her father to come home. There would be a grand fiesta in the village when the men brought the sheep down from their high pastures for the winter.

The bright day finally arrived when the people who lived in the outlying areas saw the first distant white flock pouring down the mountainside like cream and ran to ring the joyful church bell. The flocks came from every direction and converged in the big market pens on one side of the village. It was a wonder to see how the smart shepherd dogs flashed and darted like dragonflies around the sheep, keeping them together. Lastly came the husbands, fathers and brothers leading their pack burros, weary of their solitude and glad to be coming home.

The village was crowded with sheep buyers and sheep

sellers. The inn overflowed with guests and the stables were busy feeding so many horses. All the women had cooked for days in preparation for the feast to be held in the church. There would be a dance afterward on the plaza.

"Arcia, hitch up the pony," Rosa shouted out the window on that morning. "We're going in to fiesta now. Bring us those tamales you made for the church dinner. You stay here to tend the fire and milk the cow. You'll see your father when he gets home."

Arcia was very disappointed but not surprised that Rosa would not let her go to the gala dinner and the dance. Rosa hadn't let her go to the market fiesta for the last two years so she hadn't expected this year to be any different. Although she was especially sad not to see Papa as soon as he arrived, she knew it would make him unhappy to hear complaints from his family on his homecoming day. So she harnessed the pony and wished them a good time at the party. They went off in their finest dresses, Angelina and Belinda wearing great big bonnets pulled close to their faces.

The sun warmed the barn, the cat chased shadows and the morning passed quietly for Arcia. She was humming a happy little melody as she finished the chores when an elegant buggy drawn by a handsome black horse came up the road and stopped right in front of the house. The driver called to Arcia. She put down her buckets and ran to see what the woman wanted.

"I'm sorry to bother you," the beautifully dressed lady said. "I'm Doña Felicidad. I am returning home to my son at Rancho Encantado several miles from here." She paled, then passed her gloved hand over her eyes. "But I'm feeling unwell and I have used up all my medicine. I wonder if I could stop here for an hour or two to rest."

When Arcia helped Doña Felicidad down from her seat and into the house, the woman leaned heavily on her shoulder. As La Doña slumped onto Rosa's pretty quilt, she grasped

Arcia's hand and pulled her close.

"I must have medical attention immediately. Can you fetch my son—he will bring our doctor." Arcia nodded and covered La Doña with a blanket as the woman's eyes closed. When Arcia peered intently into the beautiful but ashen face, her own mouth tightened with concern. There was no time to waste. In her mind she traced the road to the great ranch. She would avoid the crowded plaza by taking a back way through the village. The little road ran four or five miles over low hills and came onto part of the vast ranch land at a wide green valley cut by a river. Everyone knew el Rancho Encantado where they raised fine cattle and horses although Arcia had never been there.

"Take my buggy," Doña Felicidad instructed. "I'll be all right until you get back. But hurry."

Arcia secured the barn and watered La Doña's black horse. Then she climbed onto the velvet-cushioned buggy seat and took up the light reins. The horse set off at a brisk trot and in less than thirty minutes they reached the town where the streets were thick with fiesta goers. People were already dancing to the violins' music and the blue smoke of roasting chili and meat hung in the air. Arcia steered the horse carefully through a narrow back street. There were many people she knew but if they saw her, they did not recognize her in the fine buggy. She caught a glimpse of her father standing among a group of men with his back toward her. Then she was out of the town and heading to the hills. The high-bred horse trotted more energetically than the sleepy pony Arcia was used to. In fact, he went at a reckless pace but when she tried to hold him back, he tossed his head impatiently and went even faster. The landscape flew by and soon the wind made Arcia's eyes blur with tears. She had never driven such a creature. The buggy's wheels bounced higher every time they struck a stone or a rut. They crested the last hill above a broad meadow where fat cattle grazed. In the valley a sun-burnished river flowed like a silver snake. Beyond the river the road continued through another velvet pasture to a copse of huge cottonwood trees. Arcia could just make out the red roofs of the ranch buildings under the shimmering leaves.

There was no doubt in the horse's mind that his dearly beloved home barn lay just ahead. Though Arcia pulled with all her strength, he whinnied joyfully and broke into a strong gallop. The buggy flew from rut to rut and swung from side to side but its terrifying banging noises only encouraged the horse to return home more quickly. Unable to hold on for one moment longer, Arcia was desperately considering how best to jump for her life when they reached the river and the horse stopped short, propelling her head over heels into the water with a huge splash.

So this is what heaven is like, she thought, certain she was dead. Then she laughed because heaven could not be so cold and wet as this. When she stood the water came only above her knees. She spit out a mouthful and took a quick inventory of her body. Thank goodness nothing was broken she thought as she wrung her sleeves. She shook the water out of her hair. The horse waited impatiently to cross, switching its silky tail at her. She took his bridle and, sloshing through the water, found he was docile enough to lead. She looked back at the high buggy seat and shivered. No, she would not sit on that for anything. She had two strong legs, she would walk to the ranch. Beside her the horse's aristocratic head bobbed as quietly as the old pony's ever had.

She shivered a little when she passed under the tall carved gate and slowly up an immaculate drive lined with poplar trees. Rosa always said rich people never had anything to do with poor farmers like them. What if they didn't believe Doña Felicidad needed help? What if they thought she was somehow to blame? When Arcia came to the long, low hacienda she went around to the back where a groom took the horse and directed her to the kitchen. Here a fat, kindly cook took her message to the estanciero. Soon she was summoned to a bright sunny room with beautiful furnishings where a handsome young man greeted her and introduced himself as Gregorio. When she told him his mother lay ill and needed a doctor, he called to his servant to hitch up the large carriage and ride for the doctor.

"I cannot thank you enough for your assistance," Gregorio said with a wide smile. It was then he noticed that Arcia's skirt was making little puddles on the polished floor. "Are you all right? You are soaked to the bone," he cried. "We must find you some dry clothing." When he clapped his hands a maid appeared.

"Please find something from Estrella's closet for this poor girl to put on," he told the woman. Turning to Arcia, he asked her how she had come to be drenched. But Arcia felt so shy she could only mumble something about the river. Gregorio smiled.

"I bet that devil ran away with you, didn't he?" he said. "It's not the first time he's done it. Did he put you in the river?"

Arcia nodded.

"Well, I'm just going to have to put my foot down with Mother. She insists on driving that horse and I have to say she handles him well. But he's too fast for a buggy." Arcia nodded again for she agreed he was much too fast, at least for her. When the maid beckoned to her she followed up the stairs and into a big room full of beautiful dolls and interesting books. She put on the dress laid out for her, rolled her wet clothes into a ball and hurried down.

"We have a few minutes to wait while the horses are harnessed," the young estanciero said handing her a cup of chocolate.

"A bocadillo? The cook has already made up a plate." So it happened that Arcia, dressed in a fine blue gingham dress dined on smoked ham and white bread and sipped chocolate from a porcelain cup in the finest house in the land. How she wished Angelina and Belinda could see her or better still, be there. But she could never even tell them about it because it would only make them angry. Full of these wonderful but confusing thoughts, she could make no reply to the young man's friendly questions except to shyly thank him for the chocolate.

Then they were in the carriage and after they picked up the doctor they came to the village. Here their passage was slowed by many people who applauded Gregorio for he was well known as a brave army officer and a generous employer. When they reached the little house by the river, Gregorio and the doctor carried Doña Felicidad into the carriage. Her eyes opened only once to gaze upon Arcia, blinked with astonishment, then closed again. With a worried look, Gregorio thanked Arcia, then lightly kissed her hand.

"The dress," Arcia stammered, plucking at the pretty skirt. Gregorio's brow wrinkled for a moment as if he were remembering something painful. Then he sighed and shook his head.

"Please keep it," he said. He glanced at the carriage where his mother lay still, waiting. "It's very becoming. We would like you to have it. To remember us by." As he swung into the carriage the springs squeaked under his weight and the horses flexed their powerful haunches, eager for the signal to go.

"Brave girl!" he cried out the window as the carraige started forward. "Some day. . ." But his words were lost in the sound and dust. Then he was gone and the air was filled with silence.

But Arcia's heart was not. Had Gregorio held her gaze a moment longer than necessary? What did he mean about 'some day'? She looked down at her broken shoes and smoothed the tucks in the bodice of the soft gingham dress. She had never had anything as nice. No, he was only being kind to a farm girl. She touched the tiny star above her eyes. It was only a dream, the lady, the carriage, the handsome man, but it was a wonderful dream and she would live on the memory for the rest of her life. What a miracle! A dress of her own. And she had even seen a little of the fiesta! But she turned now to the cow needing to be milked and the fire she must start to welcome her father home.

By the time he arrived Arcia was asleep in the hay with her
head on the gingham dress she had wrapped safely inside her
pillow.

Her father was very happy to see her the next morning and
admired the little star on her forehead which Rosa told him
she had given Arcia as a gift. Rosa also told him that Arcia had
begged to sleep with the animals, helpfully pointing out that
there was much more room in the barn than in the kitchen
by the hearth. When her father inquired why Angelina and
Belinda wore bonnets, Rosa told him they had very bad colds
and needed to keep their heads warm at all times. Arcia did not
dispute any of this since there was no hope of changing anything. Papa would have to leave again in early spring so she
might as well make his few months at home as pleasant as possible. Besides, it didn't matter where she slept because in her
dreams she wore dresses made of rainbows and danced with the
handsomest man in the kingdom.

When winter passed, her father returned to the mountains

with a large flock. Fat grey rain clouds hid those distant mountains when one day the big carriage appeared down the road. Arcia was busy as usual doing barn chores when she heard the horses stop in front of the house. With a pounding heart she watched Doña Felicidad and Gregorio alight and knock at the front door.

"Perhaps La Doña wants the dress back," Arcia thought. Suddenly Belinda ran from the house to the barn.

"Get inside and hide, quickly," she snapped, glancing around for somewhere to conceal Arcia. "They mustn't see you. Under the hay, hurry."

"Have I done something wrong?" Arcia asked, thinking how she would miss the gingham dress. But Belinda only heaped more hay over her, then left, closing the barn door behind her.

Arcia could hear the voices of people coming toward the barn. First, Rosa's voice, sharp and complaining. Then La Doña's, firm and insistent. Next, Gregorio's, deep and melodious, as he calmed Angelina and Belinda who clacked and clamored like geese.

Arcia could hear the barn door creak open.

"She was right here when we drove up," Doña Felicidad said.

"Well, she's not here now, is she?" Rosa sniffed. "Whew, I never could stand the smell of animals."

"Looks like a good clean barn to me," Gregorio replied. "Everything's in its place. Who keeps it for you?"

"Oh, little Arcia does all the chores," Rosa replied. "I don't understand why you want a barn hand for a companion, señora. One of these refined girls would do better for you. And besides, Arcia's not here. I think she's gone out with the goats today."

"Aren't those the goats in the corral?" Gregorio asked. "I'm sure she's here. Perhaps she's too shy to greet us. She was wonderfully shy when I met her. And wonderfully beautiful."

"You call that beautiful?" Rosa said. "Now these are what I call beauties. Smile, girls, and show the lady your nice curtseys." They smiled and curtseyed but the lady only sighed.

"Perhaps she isn't here, Gregorio," his mother said with disappointment. "Well, I suppose we'd better be on our way." Gregorio was patting the pony in his stall when the cat who had been sitting on the grain bin let loose a mighty yowl, leaped to the top of the haystack and began to dig like a crazy animal. To the astonishment of La Doña and Gregorio and to the dismay of Rosa and her daughters, the cat threw hay into the air until the top of Arcia's head appeared.

"Oh dear," was all Arcia could say, blushing and smiling with embarrassment because, after all, she had heard every word they'd said and besides, there was hay sticking to every part of her. "Oh dear," she repeated.

Doña Felicidad burst out laughing, helped her up and hugged her. Then she thanked Arcia for saving her life.

"While risking her own driving your racehorse, my dear Mother," Gregorio added. Arcia blushed again and reached down to stroke the little cat who was rubbing against her legs, purring loudly. It must be a dream. But it was not a dream. Now that she had recovered completely, Doña Felicidad said, she wanted to know if Arcia would consent to spend a year or so travelling with her as a companion. Not as a paid companion, more as a member of the family. Arcia was so like her darling Estrella who had died two years before. La Doña blinked and swallowed oddly when she spoke of her daughter. So, Arcia realized, it was Estrella's dress. It was clear that La Doña missed the girl very much.

Arcia looked to Rosa. "May I accept?" she asked humbly. Swiftly calculating the advantages of a connection to Doña Felicidad who might possibly invite Angelina and Belinda to a fancy ball where they would surely meet estancerios at least as rich and powerful as Gregorio, Rosa graciously nodded her head.

"And you may take your dear little kitty with you," she added, giving the cat a spiteful look.

"Or we shall drown the wretch," Angelina declared through gritted teeth.

"Hush, hush my darlings," Rosa remonstrated, stepping hard on Angelina's toes. But Doña Felicidad was not listening.

"Let us go now, my dear Arcia," Doña Felicidad was saying. "There's much preparation and a ship which departs in only two weeks. Now kiss all your family good-bye, for you'll be gone a long time." Then she and Gregorio went to wait in the carriage.

Arcia said farewell to all the animals she had cared for and packed her few belongings, including the gingham dress, into a small bag. In just a few moments she, Rosa, Angelina and Belinda were standing beside the gilded carriage.

"Good-bye Rosa and thank you for everything," Arcia said. "Please tell Papa I am safe and happy." She leaned to give Rosa a kiss on the cheek. Rosa fluttered her hands and patted Arcia's sleeve.

"Good-bye Angelina, good-bye Belinda," Arcia said and tears filled her eyes for the first time since the star fell on her. But they were different tears, they were not for herself but for her poor stepsisters. How miserable they looked, how angry and bewildered. In a sudden rush of affection for them, Arcia hugged them quickly, one after the other. Under their mother's fierce glare they endured her embrace but they turned their faces away.

Then Gregorio handed Arcia into the carriage as if she were a lady in silk instead of a ragged farm girl, pulled the gleaming door closed behind him and signalled the driver to go on. The horses leaned into their shiny collars, the wheels rumbled and with a jingle of harness bells the carriage rolled away, leaving behind only a cloud of dust. In the silence that fell, the cow bawled, the chickens clucked and the pigs squealed because it was nearly feeding time.

"Well, good riddance to bad rubbish," Belinda said, yanking loose the ribbon under her chin. "I'm glad she's gone. And I'm not wearing this hat another minute." She pulled it off and threw it into the road.

"Who needs her or this stupid hat?" Angelina declared, tossing hers into the bushes. "What good does it do?"

Rosa bent to retrieve the hats, thinking how, without Arcia, everything was changed. She straightened up and cast a realistic eye on her two bad-tempered, lazy daughters. She would have her work cut out for her just getting them to do their share. She looked more closely at Belinda and Angelina. Heavens, could she believe her eyes? Yes, yes it was true, the horn had disappeared and the donkey ears were gone!

"Look at yourselves," she cried, laughing and weeping for joy. The girls clapped their hands to their heads and ran to look in the mirror.

"They're gone!" they screamed. "We're beautiful again!" Then they stopped and thought about what they had just said.

"You're normal, anyway," Belinda said.

"Speak for yourself," Angelina snapped. "It's because Arcia's gone," she added spitefully.

"I always knew she was a witch," Belinda said. "That's why I never let her touch me."

"But it was when she hugged you that your horn and your ears went away," Rosa said with exasperation. For a long moment the daughters were very quiet, considering this. Each was thinking that if Arcia had touched her sooner, she might have been the one who drove off in the golden carriage to live happily ever after. But it was too late to do anything but finish the day as best they could. Rosa sighed. She knew they would all remember the star that fell on Arcia for a long time.

Strangely enough, the star on Arcia's forehead disappeared almost before the house was out of sight. Arcia had already forgotten all about it. She was too busy thinking about the exciting adventures which spread out before her like a banquet.

Doña Felicidad was telling her how important education was for girls to grow into strong women not unlike herself. When Gregorio shyly offered to teach her to play the piano and to drive the fine horse who had run away with her, Arcia nodded, dumb with happiness. But first, Doña Felicidad continued firmly, Arcia must settle into her new home where her own sunny room and soft warm bed awaited her. She would be the sister Estrella never had. Arcia sighed blissfully and the faithful little cat purred even more loudly in her lap. Yes, they all did live happily ever after.

Afterword

Long ago in the villages of northern New Mexico, cuentistas passed on their cultural history in the kinds of stories presented here. Their folktales strengthened the bonds of their community and enhanced their sense of identity. Although social change has nearly obliterated live storytelling, folklorists, sociologists and writers steeped in the literature of the region have recorded and collected the old tales in many learned volumes rich in historical imagery.

Such folktales may have originated in Spain but were nourished on the blood, sweat and tears of the settlers until they became the myths of a people who lived and died on New Mexican soil. There are lessons still to be learned from their traditions. One of the most important aspects of their vanishing culture is the individual's responsibility to the community, an arrangement strikingly similar to American Indians' emphasis on first loyalty to the tribe. These people recognized that they could survive only through mutual support and cooperation. In the early ejido system of commonly owned land which sustained Hispanic villages in New Mexico, everyone mattered and nothing interfered with man's primal relationship to the earth.

Credit for bringing these cuentos into book form goes to the enthusiastic editor and publisher Joe Mowrey whose tactful criticism improved every draft of every story. Much credit goes also to my tireless, exacting and loyal research assistant-editor and mate, Jim Tirjan, whose enduring faith in me finally bore fruit. And lucky the author to have an illustrator-designer like Janice St. Marie who adds imagination and artistic value to written words and puts everything together.

Many thanks to Al Regensberg at the State Archives, Orlando Romero at the Museum of New Mexico and the staff at the Santa Fe Public Library who cheerfully guided our research efforts. And to Sam Adelo, the Nances and our other good friends who took the time to read the manuscript and offered technical advice.

Reed Stevens
Santa Fe

Suggested Good Reading

"Enchantment and Exploitation; The life and Hard Times of a New Mexico Mountain Range" by William DeBuys, University of New Mexico Press, 1985.

"Hispano Folklife of New Mexico; The Lorin W. Brown Federal Writers' Manuscripts" by Lorin W. Brown with Charles L. Briggs and Marta Weigle, University of New Mexico Press, 1978.

"Literary Folklore of the Hispanic Southwest" by Auroroa Lucero-White Lea, Naylor Company, 1953.

"Folktalkes: Cuentos Espanoles de Colorado y New Mexico" University of New Mexico Press 1977, 2 volumes.

Author's note: unfortunately, not all these books are still in print but a diligent reader will find them in Southwest collections of good public or university libraries.

The Author

Reed Stevens lives in an adobe house she and her mate Jim Tirjan built in Santa Fe, New Mexico. Reed has been a radio commentator, journalist and photographer for many years. Her play, *Crazy Nora*, the story of a notorious 19th century Irish immigrant which aired on NPR Theater, sparked a deep fascination with history and myth which inspired her to interpret the old folktales you have just read.

When she is not researching or writing, Reed loves to cook and garden. She and Jim enjoy horseback riding in the beautiful Sangre de Christo mountains and the wide open spaces of New Mexico where every day is a blessing.

The Illustrator

Janice St. Marie has been an illustrator and designer since 1981. Her work has gained increased recognition and popularity throughout the Southwest and nationally. She lives in Santa Fe, New Mexico on ten piñon-covered acres with her husband, six cats, two dogs and assorted fish.

The Publisher

Mariposa Printing & Publishing was established in 1980. Our goal is to provide quality-crafted, limited edition publications in various literary fields.

Your comments and suggestions are appreciated. Contact Joe Mowrey, owner-production manager, Mariposa Printing & Publishing, 922 Baca Street, Santa Fe, New Mexico, (505) 988-5582.

Also from Mariposa Publishing

Children's Literature

By Joe Hayes

> **The Day It Snowed Tortillas**
> Tales from Spanish New Mexico
>
> **Coyote &**
> Native American Folk Tales
>
> **The Checker Playing Hound Dog**
> Tall Tales from
> A Southwestern Storyteller
>
> **A Heart Full of Turquoise**
> Pueblo Indian Tales

By Gerald Hausman

> **Turtle Dream**
> Collected Stories from the Hopi
> Navajo Pueblo, & Havasupai People
>
> **Ghost Walk**
> Native American Tales
> of the Spirit

Adult Literature

> **Sweet Salt, A Novel**
> By Robert Mayer